S0-DTA-111

BARNEY BUCK AND
THE WORLD'S WACKIEST WEDDING

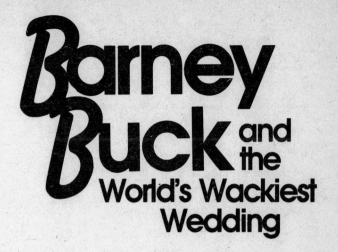

Barney Buck and the World's Wackiest Wedding

GILBERT MORRIS

WindRider BOOKS

Tyndale House Publishers, Inc., Wheaton, Illinois

TO ANDREA NICOLE SMITH

"Those that be planted

in the house of the Lord

shall flourish

in the courts of our God."

First printing, April 1986

Library of Congress Catalog Card Number 85-52181
ISBN 0-8423-0339-1
© 1986 by Gilbert Morris
All rights reserved
Printed in the United States of America

CONTENTS

ONE
Wedding Bells

Goober Hollow, Arkansas, is only about six hundred miles from Chicago, but it took us about three years to get moved. Really moved.

Oh, we made the trip in about twelve hours, but it took us a long time to get settled down. I was twelve, my brother Jake was ten, and Joe was only eight at the time, and none of us had ever set foot outside of Chicago. I guess we never would have if it hadn't been for the accident.

I'll never forget the day when our parents were supposed to pick us up after school, but instead we were met by a policeman and a lady named Miss Jean Fletcher. They tried to break the news gently, but how do you tell three kids their parents have been killed in a car wreck?

I still have bad dreams about the weeks

that followed, and I guess if it hadn't been for Miss Jean I would've gone bananas. She was appointed by the juvenile court to look after us, and she did the best she could.

They tried to find somebody to adopt all three of us, but they couldn't. That's when they decided to split us up, sending us to three different homes.

What happened then sounds like the plot of a really *bad* book, but I'll tell it the way it was.

Jake was always a pretty shrewd operator, and he found out about this old house with some land that had been our dad's old home place in Goober Hollow, back in Arkansas. He came up with the nutty scheme for us to go there and live. The court judge would never have let us do it, had we not managed to convince Miss Jean that we had relatives there who'd take us in. She sold the judge on the idea.

Believe it or not, we came to Goober Hollow and managed to convince not only the judge, but almost everybody in the county that we had parents. The truth came out eventually, and I still feel bad about all that deception we pulled on Miss Jean.

How we did it still amazes me! When we came to Arkansas, I'd never eaten grits, never worn overalls, didn't know how to run a trotline, couldn't milk a cow if my life had depended on it! We were so "green" that when Joe found a pile of old milk bottles, he thought it was a cow's nest!

But we learned, and we made some good friends that year. It was a good thing we did, because if it hadn't been for people like Coach Dale Littlejohn and Chief Potter and a few more solid citizens who went to bat for us, we'd have been dragged back to Chicago and put in different homes!

Miss Jean came down and when all these good people volunteered to sponsor us, she cried because we'd lied to her. We Bucks did some crying, too, but in the end, she went to bat for us. With her help, we got to stay on.

Now let me bring you up-to-date!

Coach Dale Littlejohn was really our best friend. He was my Sunday school teacher and my coach and was super in every way. He looked about ten times better than Robert Redford and weighed the same as he did when he was All-American cornerback at Alabama. I guess half the girls in Clark County were madly in love with him.

Miss Jean, with her golden blonde hair and true-blue eyes, looked like a fashion model. Wouldn't you know that they fell in love with each other, and decided to get married and *adopt all three of us!* That would happen *after* she got her degree from the University of Chicago.

The day before Thanksgiving I was leaning against the split-rail fence watching the pumpkins grow. The breath of fall coming off the Ouachita Mountains was tart with wood smoke, and the hardwoods were showing off their autumn colors—gold, red, and burning orange.

For weeks we'd been gathering berries and fruit, and now, thanks to Mrs. Taylor, the cellar was packed with jams, jellies, and preserves of every kind—strawberry, blackberry, muscadine, wild grape, crabapple, peach, pear, and apple. I thought of the smokehouse, crowded with bacon, hams, sausages, and other choice meats for the long winter months.

My black-and-tan hound Tim was nuzzling my leg—and was just about worn out from chasing coons all night. I was tired, too, but the thought of six fresh coon hides on stretching boards in the barn made me feel good. It would swell my college fund considerably.

Suddenly Tim raised his head and said, "Wuff!" and I got up to see who was coming down our road. When I saw Coach Littlejohn's gold Camaro and beside him Miss Jean, I let out a yell and cleared the fence like a world-class hurdler.

Coach swung the car around, throwing on the brakes and showering the house with gravel. Right away Miss Jean piled out and ran toward me, calling out, "Barney! Barney!"

I caught her and spun her around in a circle, hugging her till she squealed.

"Put me down, you brute!" she panted, then

stared up at me and shook her head. "You've *grown.*"

I didn't mind her saying that, but I'd heard so many bad jokes about how tall I was that it had gotten old. I guess the first time somebody'd said, "How's the air up there?" it was mildly funny. But after hearing it a thousand or so times, the humor had worn off.

I looked down at her and said, "No, Miss Jean, I think you're shorter. It must be that all that heavy education you've stuffed in your head has stunted your growth."

"A little more respect for Dr. Fletcher, Barney!" Coach said with a grin.

"Oh, Dale, I won't have my degree for another month."

"I can't wait," he said. Giving me a wink, he added, "Now that you know all about psychology, I guess I won't be able to fool you anymore. You'll see right through ole Dale, I reckon."

She pushed her chin out at him, which wasn't exactly the most frightening sight I ever saw, and said, "You never *could* fool me, Dale Littlejohn."

Well, I just grinned at her, because she was so crazy about him that she'd have jumped off a fire tower if he'd said to do it!

At about that time Joe and Jake came running out of the house. Jake was like our dad—short, strong, and looking a lot like an

Indian. Well, our grandmother was a quarter Cherokee, so he came by it honestly. It tickled me to see him hugging Miss Jean, because he didn't usually do that kind of thing.

Joe resembled Mom—thin with fine blond hair and eyes as blue as cornflowers. He also had dyslexia, a problem that kept him from reading. Still he was really the brain of the family. He could make machines, repair broken things, and just about do anything with his hands.

After all the hugging, we went into the house and had coffee and fresh fried pies, which were my specialty. When better fried pies are made, Barney Buck will make them, I always say.

Miss Jean downed one pie and popped another in her mouth, saying, "Mmmmmm! How I've missed these pies!"

"Keep eating like that," Coach said, "and you'll get so fat you won't be able to get through the door."

"Don't worry, Coach," I said. "She may be better looking than you, but you dress better than she does."

He turned red as he always did when I kidded him about his fancy clothes. "I've been meaning to talk to you about that foppish attire, Dad," I rattled on. "I mean, after all, we *do* have a certain position in the community, and I—*Ow!*"

He moved as quickly as a cat, and he was

the strongest man I knew. He had me out of my chair and flipped upside-down like a pillow stuffed with feathers before I even knew what was happening!

He held me by my ankles and, thumping my head on the floor, said, "Let's have a little more respect for the old man, all right?" Then he turned me up and plopped me back onto the chair.

"Dale! You might have hurt him!" Miss Jean said with a gasp.

"Woman, let's settle this right now!" he said firmly. "If any one of these three boys of ours needs a thrashing, I'm the man to see he gets it!"

"Gee!" Joe said. "That's just the way Dad always talked, wasn't it, Barney?"

Was he right! I couldn't even talk, and it sounds silly, I guess, but it made me happy to know that I'd have a dad who'd love me enough to tell me when I was wrong.

I had a lump in my throat, so I cleared it and said, "Well, Dr. Fletcher, did you find us a crash pad in Chicago? We've been talking about seeing some of our old buddies when we move back."

The plan had been to let Miss Jean finish her degree and then Coach would find a job and we'd all live there. It wasn't what I would've chosen, but to have a set of parents like *them* I wouldn't have minded living in a trash can!

"Well . . . actually, there's something I have to tell you. . . . I mean that *we* have to tell you."

My stomach started to ache, and the first thing I thought was *They've called off the wedding.*

Miss Jean was usually a pretty good talker, but now she was having trouble. "I've been meaning to write. . . . That is, I suppose I should have called. . . ."

Coach put his arm around her and grinned at us. "What she wants to say, you guys, is that she's coming to live in Goober Hollow!" Then he gave a rebel cry and picked her up, saying, "We may have lost the Civil War, but here's one Yankee girl who's learned how to sing 'Dixie'!"

Well, it was great. We all wanted to stay, and now that Miss Jean and Coach were, what could be better?

"So you're going to find a house in town and live there?" I asked.

"No, we want to move in with *you*," Coach said with a grin. "You can see what a pair of moochers you'll have for parents, can't you?"

"Move here!" I yelled. "That's great!" So we whooped and hollered some more.

We loved this old dog-trot house, with two sections to it and a big breezeway right down the middle. A dog could trot right through it, but this type of house actually was built this way because it was cooler.

"Well, I think we'll have to do a little cleaning—" I began to say, but Coach cut me off with a wave of his hand.

"Forget it," he said. "You guys keep house with a rake."

"But. . . ," I said, a bit confused.

"Dale is giving me the most wonderful present!" Miss Jean cried out with stars in her eyes. "He's going to have the whole place redecorated, inside and out!"

"Tom Clifford will be here to start the work next Monday, so you guys can pick out your wallpaper," he added.

"That's really why I came back," Miss Jean said. "I'll be finishing my work just before Christmas, and we plan to get married on the first day of the year. So we have to plan everything today."

Well, we had a great time picking out wallpaper and paint and stuff like that. Jake wanted wallpaper with pictures of The Beasts of Burden, his favorite rock group. But I convinced him that if he woke up in the night, just one glimpse of those weirdos would give him heart failure. And Joe wanted everything fire-engine red, but settled for a loud orange. I wanted a tiger skin carpet and flocked walls, but they laughed at that for some reason.

Finally Coach got it all down, and I was walking back to the car with him while Miss Jean said good-bye to Jake and Joe.

"By the way, Coach, where will the wedding be?" I asked.

He looked a little sad then and said, "That's the only thing that's not perfect about this whole thing, Barney. I'm spending every dime I have on this house, so there's no money for a big wedding."

"Maybe she doesn't want one."

"Yes, I'm afraid she does. Her sister told me that the biggest dream of Jean's life has been to have a real fancy wedding." Then he shrugged and added, "Her father's dead, you know, and she's spent all her savings on getting this Ph.D. So, it looks like we'll have to settle for the pastor's study."

Then all of a sudden I had this absolutely *brilliant* idea!

Usually Jake got these great ideas, but for once in my life I was inspired.

Miss Jean was approaching the car with Jake and Joe hanging onto her, and I said loudly, "I have an announcement to make!"

"You're going to start taking baths again?" Jake asked. He had this perverted sense of humor which I ignored.

"Miss Jean, you have been helping us out for three long years," I said carefully. "I don't know what we would have done without you."

"Oh, Barney—"

"Please hear me out. For a long time we've looked for a way to show you how much we appreciate what you've done for us, and I am happy to announce that the time has came."

"That should be the time has *come,* shouldn't it, Barney?" Jake whispered, and I shut him down by digging my elbow into his ribs. You can't reason with a kid!

"What we want to do is give you . . . for your wedding gift. . . ." I took a deep breath, then let it roll out slowly and with great force. "We are going to give you the most splendid, the most bodacious, the most exciting and beautiful and most anything-else-you-can-think-of wedding this town has ever seen!"

And Jake, not to be outdone, added, "And a honeymoon to match!"

Of course Coach and Miss Jean argued about it, said we couldn't afford it, but I was stubborn as a mule.

"When you adopt us, whatever you say goes," I said firmly, "but we're going to have our own way in this one thing. So you go get your degree, and we'll take care of invitations, preachers, flowers, rice, clothes, music, decorations, notices, and all the rest of it."

"We really shouldn't let you do it," Miss Jean said as she got into the car.

"It'll be the biggest thing this county has ever seen!" I said grandly. "Why, I'll bet for years people will say things like 'That happened the year before the Littlejohns' wedding,' or maybe 'Our baby cut his first tooth the same month that Dale and Jean had that great wedding.' "

"Barney, if you need help on it, come to me," Coach said.

But I didn't even respond. I was saying something that Jake quoted to me several times before the thing was over: "Yep, people will be saying, 'I never saw *anything* like that wedding the Buck boys put on!' "

TWO
High
Finances

We had a great Thanksgiving, and then Miss
Jean flew back to Chicago. Coach went to see
his folks in Texas, and we were left to figure
out a way to make a lot of money in less than
a month.

Early Friday morning, we had a council of
war at the breakfast table. "The first thing
we need to do—" I began, but Jake took over.

"Here's the figure, Barney," he said,
throwing a sheet of paper in front of me.
"I've listed all the expenses we'll need to take
care of, and I think you'll find my figures
will be pretty accurate."

Since the whole thing had been *my* idea, I
thought I would be in charge, but I should
have known Jake better than that!

"Let's see that paper," I snapped. "You don't

l now a thing about weddings. . . . What!" I jumped up from the table and waved the paper under Jake's nose.

"What's wrong, Barney?" Jake asked. "Did I make a mistake?"

"You're out of your tree, Jake Buck!" I screamed at him. "Three thousand dollars! It's–it's *obscene!*"

"I thought you wanted to go first class," he said calmly, staring at me with those black beady eyes of his. "It never occurred to me that you'd want to be a welcher and give the folks a shoddy wedding."

He certainly has a way with words, that brother of mine. I felt like a sheep-killing dog, but I went on anyway. "Well, I *don't* want a shoddy wedding, but good night! For a thousand dollars we ought to be able to get the New York Symphony to play at the thing!"

"Noooo," Jake said calmly, "that would cost more, but if you think it would be a good idea—"

"Never mind!" I yelled. "Just let me see that list. There *must* be a way to cut down!"

"You get what you pay for, Barney," Jake said with a shrug.

"How much do we actually have, Barney?" Joe asked. "I mean if you added up all our savings and all the stuff we can sell and what we have in the checking account, what would the *whole* thing come to?"

"Twenty-six dollars and thirty-five cents," Jake said promptly. "I already added it up."

"My stomach hurts," I said feebly. "Why did you guys let me get into this mess?"

Jake was cool. "Oh, don't fuss and carry on like that, Barney. Something will turn up."

That rang a bell. I sat up and stared at Jake. He looked innocent enough, but I knew something was incubating in that head of his.

"You're on to something, aren't you?" I said, pointing my finger at him. "You've got one of your fruitcake ideas! Don't lie to me, Jake Buck. I know that look!"

Joe jumped up. He was still young enough to get excited about Jake's schemes. "What is it, Jake?" he asked excitedly. "You have to tell us!"

Jake shook his head. "No, I've got to work on it a little more."

"Well, we can't raise this kind of money by raking leaves—not in a month," I snapped. "We'll have to trim this list."

"Nothing on there but essentials," Jake argued. "That is, if you meant what you said to Coach and Miss Jean."

I stared at the list hypnotized, then said, "Well, what about this cost for flowers—five hundred bucks!"

"Got that figure from Williams. He ought to know."

We went over the list item by item, and no matter how we cut it, three thousand dollars was what it was going to take.

"Course we don't have to send them to Biloxi for a honeymoon," Jake finally said in disgust. "We can send them out to the truck stop and let them listen to the drivers talk! I guess you'd approve of that since it wouldn't cost anything."

"Wait a minute," Joe said, and he put a hand on both of us. Joe hated arguments. "Let's don't fight about it. I think we ought to work together. And Barney . . . ," he turned to me and added, "you said last night when we were reading our chapter in the Bible that we have not because we ask not. Why don't we just ask God to help us!"

"God helps those that help themselves!" Jake said righteously. "I think that's in the book of James."

"It's in *Aesop's Fables!*" I said. "And every time I hear people say that, I know they're bound and determined not to have faith."

"OK! OK!" Jake threw up his hands. "I'm just trying to get this thing going. If you want to do it by faith, it suits me fine."

"Jake," I said, "I'm not against doing everything we can, but I think this is one of those times when the job is just too *big* for us. So let's pray like we wouldn't get the money any other way, and then let's work the same way—like it all depended on us."

Jake grinned. "I think your theology is sound, brother. And as soon as my plan is ripe, I'll let you in on it."

For a couple of days all three of us worked our fingers to the bone doing everything that earned a dollar or two. Yard work, painting, delivering for the lumber company—we took anything that came our way.

But it was no use and we all knew it. If we had a year to raise the money, it would have been possible, but there was no time. I mentioned using the college fund, but Coach found out about the idea and set his foot down, so that was that.

I guess everyone has a place to go to when he wants to do some heavy thinking. Mine was over at the edge of our house not far from the Caddo River. I got up and ate an early breakfast; then Tim and I made our way to a spot under some tall pines right beside an old logging road that crossed the woods.

For a long time I wandered through the woods, letting Tim chase squirrels. When a cold breeze came up off the river, I decided it was time to build a fire.

I gathered up a bunch of tiny sticks no larger than toothpicks and made a little tepee out of them, then put some dry pine branches over them and then some heavier pieces of dead hickory limbs over those. As I touched off the fire and watched it catch like something soaked in coal oil, I smiled to think how easily I'd done it—and how hard it had been for me to build a fire when I'd first come to live in the woods.

For about an hour, I sat there feeding the fire, thinking about how good life was to us, especially the part that lay ahead—having a mom and dad again. And having that fancy wedding!

I racked my brain trying to figure out a way to afford the best for Coach and Jean, but I knew it was hopeless unless a miracle came along. I did something then that Coach didn't really approve of. I took out my New Testament, let it fall open, and stuck my finger on a verse in Matthew.

Coach had said, "That's the Lucky Dip method, Barney. I don't think you ought to make any serious decisions on a method like that. Study! That's the way to learn how to follow Jesus!"

I didn't really have any confidence in that way of finding out what to do either, but I looked down at the verse my finger was on and I nearly jumped straight up into the air!

Right under my finger were the words: "Ask, and it shall be given you. . . ."

To tell the truth, I got a little nervous. I really wanted Miss Jean to have her wedding, but at the same time I was leery about asking God for *things*. It had always seemed a little selfish to me. But I sat there reading the verse over and over again, and then I read a bit more: "If ye then, being evil, know how to give good gifts unto your children, how much more shall your Father which is in heaven give good things to them that ask him?"

24

I closed the New Testament, put it back in my pocket, and had a little talk with God, mostly telling him I didn't want the money for *me* but for Coach and Miss Jean. I guess I didn't have much faith when I finally got up, but what little I had I made up my mind to use.

It was about eight o'clock and I had to help old Mrs. Taylor take down some shelves, so I whistled for Tim and started to go home.

But Tim didn't show up, which was unusual. I called him and then heard him barking. I followed him to a flat spot of ground just at the edge of the woods. He was digging as hard as he could to get something out of a hole near a fallen oak.

"Come on, Tim," I said. "That's probably just an old armadillo. We have to go."

But he kept at it so hard I thought it might be a fox or something, so I chambered a shell in my .22 and got ready in case it was. A good fox hide would bring a pretty fair price.

I leaned over and pulled at the old tree, which was so brittle it came loose in my hand and I fell over backward. A big armadillo came scooting out from under the tree and scurried off, making me wish for the millionth time that armadillos had hides. I was scrambling to my feet when my foot hit something hard. No stones were usually found in this part of the country, just red clay, yet when I leaned over, there was a sharp edge of a big rock.

"What in the world. . . ?" I put my gun down and tried to pick up the rock, but it was stuck in the ground. Then I noticed a funny thing: it wasn't a native stone. It was smooth like quarried stone. As I leaned closer, I saw that under all the clay dirt there were letters carved in the face of it!

Well, I made the dirt fly and in a few minutes I had it out. It was a triangular shape and the letters were rough—different from the ones on tombstones.

I scraped away the dirt until the letters were fully exposed, but they didn't make any sense. Part of each side was broken off, and I tried to find the other pieces, without success. No matter how I tried to get some meaning out of the letters, it was no use. I made a drawing of the stone on a pad I always kept in my pocket, and it looked like this:

```
        T E R S O
         O L I D
       S E  U M A
      M P O R I U
```

I wanted to take it home, but it was too heavy, so I pulled the old log over it and just for curiosity started poking around, digging with a sharp stick.

I guess I was hoping to find some more carved pieces, but I didn't. What I did find was a lot of pottery fragments. That excited me, because I'd been doing some archaeology reading, and I knew that those professors always find pottery at the sites where they dig up old cities.

Some of the fragments had marks, but I couldn't read them, and then just as I was getting ready to go home I found something really exciting.

I was poking around a big ash tree where the fallen leaves had built up a thick blanket of mulch, when my stick hit something! I threw the stick away and went at it with my hands, and in a minute I realized I had hit a big bone. It was huge! I yanked it out and stood there staring at it, knowing it hadn't come from any animal I knew. It was about six feet long with knobs on both ends, but it was at least three or four inches thick.

"It's a fossil!" I said right out loud. "It's got to be because it's so big!"

Well, I stood there staring at the thing, wondering what to do with it.

First, I thought about going to Mr. Simpson, the biology teacher at the high school. But all the time an idea was building up in my mind.

I guess those books I'd been reading on archaeology had made a bigger impression than I knew, because all of a sudden I realized that this was a valuable find! Why some of the stuff they'd taken out of tombs in Egypt was worth millions! Of course, this was different, but I knew museums paid big bucks for things like this. Who knew what that mysterious stone might be? Maybe a relic from a lost civilization!

I decided to go home, but first hid the bone until I could get back. Then as I started back to town, I thought about the prayer I'd prayed and how I'd stumbled onto this buried stuff. There was no way I could keep from putting the two together, so by the time I got to town, I had a Master Plan that was every bit as wild and weird as anything my brother Jake had ever dreamed up!

I knew that if there *was* anything valuable in that ground, I'd have to own it or control it to make the money. Maybe some of Jake's business ability had gotten into me by osmosis, because I was a real operator that day, and by the time the sun set, I had discovered that Charlie Ott owned the land. I leased it from him for two years for one hundred dollars, which amazed him because he hadn't ever hoped to make a cent from it by farming or grazing. I let him go with the idea he came up with: "Gonna try a little goat ranchin', are you, Barney? Ought to be good for that. Won't grow nothing but weeds."

I scraped up the money, got Mr. Davis to draw up an agreement, and by the time I got home that night, I was totally exhausted.

"What you been doing all day, Barney?" Jake asked as I fell into bed.

"Oh, making our million, Jake, making our million."

He thought it was funny, but I really believed it!

I lay awake for a long time, my head spinning as I tried to figure out how to go about cashing in on the find. Finally, I dropped off to sleep, but I had a lot of bad dreams. One was about a huge hairy mammoth with thousand-dollar bills stuck on his tusks. I was trying to pull them off, and he kept stomping me. When I woke up the next morning, I felt sore all over.

Getting rich is a drag!

THREE
Turning On
the Charm

"Well, you can stop worrying, you guys." Jake plopped down on his chair at the dining room table and raked enough eggs onto his plate to feed a small African village. He looked like a cat who'd just eaten a juicy mouse, and there was that touch of arrogance he had when he was wheeling and dealing.

"What is it this time?" I asked, yawning wide. I was tired from my lack of sleep, and since I figured *my* find was going to pull us through, I wasn't too excited.

"This is no nickel-and-dime stuff, Barney! We'll clear all we need for the wedding and maybe a little fat left for yours truly."

He kept cramming eggs, sausage, and biscuits down his throat without missing a word. I don't think Jake actually *tasted* anything in his whole life!

"Well?" I asked.

"You know that big old house the Abbotts bought?"

"Sure."

Joe piped up, "We're going to build a chimney for them, Barney!"

"A chimney?" I stared at them, then said, "You guys don't know anything about building chimneys."

"Then why are the Abbotts hiring us to do the job, I ask you?" Jake shot right back. "We already got a contract, Barney, and it's gonna bring us a *bundle!*"

"You never laid a brick in your life, Jake. And besides that, you have to have smoke shelves and all kinds of fancy things."

"No sweat," Jake said casually. "This is how it came up. I heard that they were going to have to spend *thousands* of dollars to have this huge chimney built right in the middle of the house. It was really a terrible job, Barney. So what I did was to take Joe over there and he came up with a neat way to do the job at a fraction of the cost. Why, the Abbotts practically fell on our necks with gratitude!"

"Come on, Barney!" Joe said. "You have to go see what we're doing."

"I can't go, not today."

"Why not, Barney?"

"Got to go over to Conway on business."

"What kind of business?" Jake asked, but I wasn't ready to let him in on it, so I just stalled.

But Joe kept begging. So after I got dressed up in my best suit, I drove them over to the Abbott place. Jake kept looking at my suit. Finally, he said, "Well, if you drop dead, Barney, we won't have to do a thing to you."

He was dying to find out why I was going to Conway, but I had sense enough not to say anything. It even sounded crazy to me in the cold light of day.

Joe pulled me into the house, a big old mansion built back before 1900. It had two stories with a high-pitched roof and the ceilings were all twelve feet high. When they showed me the big living room where the fireplace was to go, I said, "That flue will have to be thirty feet high!"

"More than that, almost forty," Joe said. "But we got it figured out, all right. See, they were going to have to tear big holes through the ceilings and put down a lot of concrete for footings, then put in thousands of bricks."

"Well, that's what it takes for fireplaces, isn't it?" I asked.

"Not this one!" Jake was beaming. He pulled a set of plans out of a drawer in a table and spread them out. "Look, what we do is take a steel pipe eight inches in diameter, we let it rest on the ground on a concrete pad, and then we cut a hole and run it right through the house, all the way up through the attic and out the roof."

I stared at the drawing, and it really made

sense. "This is a neat blueprint. Where'd you get it?"

"Mr. Speers drew it for us," Joe said. "He charged us only twenty dollars."

"But how do you handle a pipe that long? Won't it weigh a lot?"

"Simple." Jake spread his hands out and shrugged as if he'd invented the whole thing instead of Joe. "Put in short sections, and have a welder put them together."

I stared at the plan. "Joe, will this thing really work?"

"Sure it will, Barney," Joe said with a smile. "A brick layer will just case in the pipe, and it'll look real good. The Abbotts want to use old cast-iron stoves, so we'll have an elbow on each floor. And that'll be simple."

"Well, it *looks* good," I said slowly. "When are you going to finish it?"

"We pour the slab to hold up the pipe today, put the pipe in tomorrow," Joe said. "Ted Barker will be here to put the pipes in place and do the welding."

"And we get paid right then," Jake added with a grin. "The Abbotts said they'd take care of the brick work."

"Well, guess it'll work if you say so, Joe." I smiled at him and pulled the truck keys out of my pocket. "I'll be back when you see me coming."

Jake followed me out to the car, trying to get a piece of my action, but I pulled out and left without spilling my secret.

Conway was only a couple of hours away—Interstate 40 all the way, and I pulled into the parking lot of the college about ten o'clock. The students were milling around between classes, and I stopped a fat guy wearing a pair of thick glasses. "Which way to the Science Building?" I asked.

"Right there." He pointed to a three-story red brick building to my left, then took off.

I went inside and found a board giving the names of the professors and their offices, and then I climbed up to the third floor. There was a frosted glass door with *Museum* printed in fading gold leaf. When I went inside, I found myself in an enormous room with stuffed animals everywhere, including a giraffe. The walls were lined with oak cabinets with glass tops. They held all kinds of dead bugs and stuff like that, all neatly labeled. Joe would have loved it, but I was here for business.

I saw a little man dressed in dirty white coveralls, so I said, "Hey, buddy, you know where I can find Professor Vandiver?"

The man was bending over a table, doing something on a plate. I walked across the room and peered over his shoulder. He was cutting up a fish with fancy steel knives.

He didn't even look up, so I figured he was hard of hearing. I slapped him on the back and said, "I asked where I could find Professor Vandiver."

The knife must have slipped, because the fish slid out of the tray and onto the top of the table, then off onto the floor.

"You clumsy ox!" The voice didn't belong to a *guy*—I soon found out. I found myself looking at the maddest girl I'd seen in a long time!

"Look what you've done! I spend hours getting this specimen just right, and you ruin it in one second!"

"Hey, I'm sorry!" I said. "Here, let me help you—"

"Just go away!" she said, bending over and picking up the fish. She flicked it into a steel waste container, then she started slamming her knives and stuff around.

"Look," I said, "I didn't mean to ruin your work. All I wanted was—"

"It's that way. If you'd used your *eyes*, you would've seen the professor's office without knocking innocent people around!"

She was wearing big horn-rimmed glasses, and her dark eyes were really sending off sparks. She looked about my age, but her black hair was pulled into what I'd call an old-fashioned bun. I noticed she was wearing what Debra Simmons called "old ladies shoes" that made feet look deformed.

"Well, I'm sorry," I said again, but I saw she wasn't going to talk, so I went to the door at the far end of the room. It had *Professor Socrates Vandiver* in fresh paint, and I gave a loud knock.

"Come in."

I went in and saw a desk piled high with books and a slender man wearing glasses with lenses thick as the bottom of Coke bottles. He had light brown hair that wasn't any too clean, and all over his front were the remains of breakfast—maybe from last week. He got up and came around the desk, and I noticed he was only about 5′8″.

He spoke with a funny accent, and I could tell he was in a pretty short-tempered mood, so I made my pitch.

"Professor, I read an article in the *Arkansas Gazette* last Sunday. I've been reading about archaeology, and I want to tell you how glad I am that you've come all the way to Arkansas."

The article had told how Dr. Socrates Vandiver was perhaps the best archaeologist in the world! He'd come from some big university in Germany to spend a year at the State University in Conway—mostly to dig around in old Indian mounds.

"Thank you," he said with a nod, then scowled. "Now, I am very busy . . ."

"Sure, but can I ask you to take a look at this?"

"What is it?"

I opened my schoolcase I'd brought along, took out the paper with the sketches I'd made of the fragment of stone, and handed it to him. "Can you tell me anything about this, Professor?"

He held the paper up close to his eyes, peered at it, then went over and sat down in his chair. I didn't say a word, and after what seemed like a long time, he asked, "Where did you find this?"

"Over close to Cedarville—about a hundred miles south of here."

"Did you find anything else—any more stones?"

"Lots of stuff that looks like pottery. I couldn't find the other parts of that stone."

"I see. ... ." He stared at the drawing, then finally said, "Well, it may be a find, but I can't tell anything from this." He gave the paper back and said, "Perhaps you can bring the stone itself. Well, I must get to work. . . ."

I knew I had to nail him fast, so I said, "Professor, I didn't want to mess around too much. All the books I've read about archaeology say that lots of valuable specimens are ruined by amateurs fooling around."

"Yah, that is right!"

"So there was one more thing I found, and I didn't know what to make of it."

His eyes gleamed faintly behind his thick glasses. "And what was that?"

"It was the biggest bone I've ever seen in my life!"

He jumped to his feet. "Bone! What sort of bone? Describe it to me!"

I thought he was hooked, so I didn't give too much away. "Well, it was at least five or six feet long and about three or four inches thick. I've seen every kind of bone from animals around here—cows, horses—and it's not any of those. So what is it? I thought maybe you could come and take a look at what I've found."

He stared at me, pursed his lips, then said, "Who owns this ground where you have found these things?"

I grinned at that, for he had some business sense.

"Well, if you mean who has the ground leased for two years. . . . You're looking at him!"

He gave an unexpected smile, then nodded. "I see you are a knowing young man." He stared at me, nodded again, and said, "I will come."

"Great! When?"

"Tomorrow." He walked over to the door, pulled it open, and said something that sounded like "Zantippi." *That can't be right*, I thought.

Then the girl in the white overalls came in and gave me a glare. "Yes, father?" she said, still sounding irate.

"Tomorrow we will go meet this young man at a place where he will tell you. See to the car and make sure we find it." He nodded at me and said, "Xanthippe will make the arrangements. I will see you tomorrow."

He darted out the door, and I asked her, "What did he call you?"

She looked at me as if I were a garbage man. "I'll have to spell it for you," she said, as if she were Mr. Rogers and I was a five year old. I wanted to punch her out, but I knew that wasn't right.

"My name is spelled *X-a-n-t-h-i-p-p-e,* and it's pronounced *zan-tippi.*"

"Gosh, what a rotten break for you!" I said without thinking.

Her eyes snapped. "She was the wife of Socrates, but I don't suppose you would have heard of him in this backwoods place!"

That made me mad! She was just about as big as a cricket, but she talked as if everybody in the world was dumb except for her.

"My name is Barney Buck—"

"What a rotten break for you!" she said with a tight smile.

I had to gag it down, but I made myself smile back. I'd been told I had this nice smile, but it just bounced off her like a bullet against case-hardened steel.

"Yeah, that's right," I managed to say real cool. "Well, let me show you how to get to Cedarville, and we can decide on when to meet."

"I've already decided that," she said firmly. "We'll meet at exactly nine o'clock. You tell me where to be with the truck, and don't be late."

I snapped to attention, clicked my heels together, then gave a snappy Nazi salute.

"*Yahwohl!*" I said, suddenly feeling stupid.

Why did I do a dumb thing like that? I wondered.

She turned red, and in a voice cold as Iceland asked, "Where will the meeting be?"

I had brought a map of Arkansas, and I traced her way with a blue pencil. "You'll get off the freeway on the second exit, right by a big Stuckey's shop. I'll be there to take you to the place." I tried to make amends for acting like a nerd. "I'm really glad to have this chance to meet you folks. . . ."

She turned her nose up and said, "I'm sure you are." Then she put the map into her pocket, and without saying another word, she zipped out, leaving me very much alone.

"Perfect!" I said out loud to a stuffed anteater that was staring glassy-eyed at me. "Did you see how tactfully I handled that little affair!" He just kept staring, and I patted his hairy little head. "What is this power I have over girls? I must use it only for good!"

Then I said good-bye, and there was considerably more friendliness in the eyes of the anteater than there had been in the eyes of Xanthippe Vandiver!

FOUR
The Big
Blast

At nine on the dot the next morning I was waiting at Stuckey's. I had even found somebody to help with the digging, and I felt pretty good about it.

Tiny Pringle was about seventeen or eighteen—nobody knew for sure. He had been abandoned by some carnival people when he was about three years old. Maybe his parents had died, or else somebody had recognized that he wasn't very bright and had dumped him on the town.

The welfare people had put him with a family that specialized in making a home for kids like him, and he became part of the town. He went to school long after it became obvious that he'd never get much beyond the fourth- or fifth-grade level.

It was neat the way the kids at school

looked out for Tiny, and he was never any trouble for any of the teachers. He'd sit for hours struggling through a Dick and Jane book or writing in his Redhorse notebook, the kind with big spaces between the lines. He'd just saw away with his stub of a pencil, not really writing, but he liked to think he was.

He was staying with an elderly couple named Mullins, and it was a good deal for both of them. If they hadn't had Tiny around, I think they'd have given up and gone into a nursing home. Tiny took care of the chickens, milked and fed the cow, cut firewood, and just kept the place going. Coach told me that the Mullinses, who didn't have any children, had left the place to Tiny in their will. That was a good deal for him, too.

He was finishing the breakfast I'd bought him—well, actually he was finishing *two* breakfasts, because as he said with a grin when I asked him if he wanted one egg or two, "Shoot, Barney, I don't never dirty up my plate for less than *four!*"

He was a fine-looking fellow, about 6'1" and very trim and muscular. He had light brown hair and heavy eyebrows over his warm brown eyes, and he almost always had a smile on his face. He had good teeth and a nice tan from being outside all the time. As a matter of fact, he was much better looking than I was, but then who wasn't?

Sometimes a sad thing would happen, though. When a new kid moved to town, he would warm up to Tiny. It always went bad, though, especially with the girls who were taken by his good looks and manners. Pretty soon they'd discover that he was very simple. And some of the guys dropped him when they found out. It used to make me mad, but that's the way some people are.

Anyway, I was glad to get the work for Tiny, and he was always happy to do things for people. I figured he would be just what they needed.

A big Ford Bronco XLT, so new the nubbins were still on the tires, pulled into the parking lot. Xanthippe was driving. I got out and Tiny followed me as I went over.

"Good morning, professor," I said. "You're right on time."

"Naturally!" Xanthippe snapped. "Well, are you going to wait all day? We have *important* things to do when we get through with this nonsense!"

I wanted to bop her with my Ford Tractor cap, but I forced a grin and said, "Right! Hey, this is Tiny Pringle. He's going to help you with the digging."

Professor Vandiver nodded and said, "Good. Now we go, yes?"

"You lead the way," Xanthippe said to me. She looked at my '57 GMC pickup with the home-built flatbed and said, "It can't be too far if you're going in *that*."

"Let's go, Tiny," I said, and we got into my truck and took off toward the site.

"They seem like nice people, Barney," Tiny said with a broad grin.

"Sure, Tiny," I said, thinking, *You'd think Genghis Khan and his crowd were real nice people!*

We arrived at the site, and Miss Sunshine said, "Show us where you found the artifacts."

I led them to the stone, and the professor got down on his knees and bent over it. He was scraping at it with a little knife and muttering under his breath.

"Show me where you found the bone," Xanthippe said curtly. I wanted to tell her the magic words were *please* and *thank you,* but I just took her over to the place and said, "There it is."

She glanced at the bone that I uncovered and said, "All right. You can go now."

I stared at her. "What did you say?"

She looked at me and said very slowly, "I said you can go now. You'd be in the way here."

She was wearing a pair of baggy jeans and a plaid shirt that was so long it reached to her knees. No alligators on the shirt for this one! I didn't pay much attention to how girls dressed, but this one seemed to be trying to qualify for the Annual Ugly Contest they have every year at Bucksnort.

I kept staring at her, then said, "Tiny knows where to find me in case you want to get in touch."

"Don't hold your breath," she said, and I realized that for some reason she was *trying* to make me mad. Why, I couldn't say, but it made me get stubborn the way I do sometimes.

People can pretty much get me to do almost anything, as long as they don't *push* at me. Well, for some reason this girl with the fool name was out to make me mad, so I just naturally decided she wasn't going to do it. I made up my mind to snow her until she felt like a pancake with syrup poured all over it.

It was pretty hard to find something nice to say, but I gave her my best smile and said, "You sure do have a good voice, Xanthippe."

She really did, but the minute I said it she turned almost pale, like she'd swallowed a frog or something.

"And that black hair of yours is really something, you know? I've always liked real black hair."

She seemed to be choking on something, and the mouth works sure shut down. She hadn't done a thing but say nasty things from the first minute I'd seen her, but now she was really paralyzed.

Finally, she said, "You–you can go now." But said it without much energy this time.

"All right," I drawled. "I'll see you after a while. Maybe we can go get a soda or hit the flick."

You'd have thought I'd asked her to jump into a pit of timber rattlers the way she clammed up. Then she turned her back, which was real *stiff*, and I left knowing that I could handle this one!

I gave the professor my number, told Tiny to stay with them, then left for town. I went straight to the Abbott place, and were things humming!

A big black steel pipe was in place already and was welded where two joints met. I found Joe and Jake up on the roof where the pipe was sticking out of a square hole. It stuck up about three feet in the air. I asked, "How are you going to fix the roof so it doesn't leak?"

Jake shrugged. "That's the carpenter's problem. Our job is about done. How's it look, Barney?"

"All right, I guess. Can I help?"

"Yes, we need some stuff hauled," Jake said. He turned to Joe and asked, "How about we go pick up the hardware and get it set, Joe?"

"Then we could try it out tomorrow," Joe said with a nod.

We got into the truck, and Jake spent the whole trip trying to squeeze my secret out of me. I just grinned and said, "You're not the only one in this family to have some big ideas, Jake!"

We pulled in beside the old barn Joe used for his lab and went inside. It was crammed full of junk. "Put this stuff in the truck, will you?" Joe said, tossing stuff at us.

Jake and I carted it all out, and then I asked, "This stuff—what's it for, Jake?"

"We got to fill up the bottom of the tube," he explained. "It's hollow all the way to the ground, and Joe wants to pack it up to ground level with this heavy iron stuff, then put a little cement on top of it."

"Why?"

"I don't know," Jake commented, "but I guess he knows what he's doing."

That seemed right enough, so we filled the bed of my pickup with all kinds of heavy metal stuff—nuts, doorknobs, old window sash weights—until the springs were sagging.

"Better not put any more in, Joe," I said. "We might break a spring."

"We have enough," he answered. "Let's get back and load it in."

We drove back to the Abbott house, and it was hard work hauling that stuff up to the roof. Finally, we made a sling, and I stood on the roof and hauled the stuff up in several empty five-gallon paint cans to keep it all from rolling off the roof.

"That's all of it, Barney," Joe called out.

"Good! My arms are about pulled loose, and my stomach thinks my throat's been cut. Let's go get some grub."

We went to the Sonic Drive Inn and stuffed ourselves on foot-long coney dogs and fried onions.

We got back to the Abbott place, but the welding wasn't finished, so we couldn't fill the pipe up with the scrap metal.

"Shoot!" Joe complained. "We really need to get that stuff in, but I have to go study with Mr. Simms this afternoon."

"Yeah, and I got to practice with my group," Jake said.

He thought he could play the drums, and he had some "group" that was going to make him rich and famous. Too bad they suffered under the illusion that what they were making was music. Practicing was about the only discipline he ever showed, though, so I thought he ought to keep it up.

"I'll take care of it," I offered. "Got nothing to do until. . . ."

Jake noticed I stopped, and he said, "Until *what*, Barney? What's the big mystery? You got something going, and I think it's a shame you won't let your very own brother in on the deal!"

He always forgot that *he* never let *anyone* in on his deals!

"I just dump the iron down the pipe soon as the welding's done?" I asked, ignoring Jake's comments.

"Right," Joe said. "Then tomorrow we can put a little cement on top of it, and that's that!"

"I think I can handle the job," I said. "You two can do the cement work tomorrow."

They took off, and I spent most of the day taking care of errands in town. I had to go by the hardware store, Safeway, the post office, and about five other places. I was thinking how much easier life would be when we had *parents* to take care of stuff like that!

It was six when I got back to the Abbott place, and nobody was there. The Abbotts were in Little Rock visiting Mrs. Abbott's mother, so the place was deserted.

I went up to the roof and got ready to pour the scrap in, but I decided to use buckets to pour it. I picked up one bucket, mostly filled with little stuff, and it was pretty easy to get it up high and pour it down the pipe. But the other bucket was almost too heavy. The window weights must have weighed five pounds apiece, and there was lots of other junk. I nearly dropped the second, then finally managed to get it on the lip of the pipe. When I turned it upside down, the contents went rattling down the pipe.

And then it happened. I hadn't known what was in the bottom of that steel tube. The only ones who did were Joe and Jake, and they were running madly toward the Abbott house trying to get there before I dropped that steel and iron down the maw of that pipe.

When I was up on the roof, all I knew was that that last load was so heavy that when it fell, I just sort of staggered away and fell down against one of the gable ends. It's a good thing I did, too!

I no sooner hit the roof than there was the last rattle as the iron slid down to what turned out to be dynamite. The first bucketful of metal must've been too light to touch it off. But one of those heavy sash weights did the job!

There was a rumble and I felt the whole house shake! I started to get up, but then the whole sky lit up like a cherry sky rocket and the house shook so much that I fell down. If there hadn't been a TV antenna to grab hold of, I'd have fallen to the ground and brained myself!

I once heard a tornado about a mile away—it sounded like a freight train gone crazy! Well, that's what this sounded like.

I was just about blind from the blast that poured out of that pipe, and then the sound that followed as all that steel went sailing into the sky was awful!

Some of the steel went whipping around, screaming like a ricochet from a three ought six, and there was this big *Boom* that rattled every window in town! The whole house shook and I expected it to fall down at any second.

Of course, I didn't have the foggiest idea what had happened. I thought it was the end of the world, and I was glad I was prayed up!

Then I got some of my vision back, and the ringing in my ears eased enough for me to hear Jake and Joe screaming my name.

"Barney! Barney! Where are you?"

"Here! I'm up here!" I yelled, then scrambled down to the ground as soon as I could. "What is going on!" I shouted.

"It's the dynamite!" Joe cried out. "Are you all right?"

"I–I guess so." I got the shakes then, as if I'd been in a bad car wreck. I had to sit down before I fell down. "Wh–what happened?"

"Barney," Joe said, "we were having a milkshake at the Diary Queen, and we were coming over to see how you were getting along. Well, I just happened to ask Jake if he had moved any of my dynamite caps."

"Your *what?*" I asked.

"Oh, the bunch I got from Billy Rondell. His dad works for the railroad."

"What do they use them for?"

"They clamp them on the track, Barney, when they need to signal a train to stop. And when the wheel hits it, it explodes and the conductor stops the train. It's for emergencies."

"And you had some of them?"

"A bunch! And I had stripped all the covers off and put them on the table in my lab. And Barney, that dynamite looked like little pieces of mortar, just like old mortar that's fallen out of an old chimney or a brick wall."

"Well, what happened to it, Joe?" I asked sternly.

"That's just it. Jake thought it was mortar,

and when we were getting the sand and concrete ready to pour the slab under the pipe, he raked it into a sack."

"And did what with it?" I was starting to see the awful light.

Joe lowered his head, then finally muttered, "He–he mixed it with the rest of the cement I was making in a little wooden box."

"You mean at the bottom of that pipe was a layer of live *dynamite!*" I couldn't believe it, but I had to, didn't I?

"Yes. That's what it was, Barney. All it needed was one lick of that stuff and watch out!"

Well, we weren't there long before we heard the sirens.

Lots of sirens!

Our volunteer firemen had power sirens and fancy lights on their pickups. They took a lot of pride in how fast they could get to a fire, and I didn't have to guess why they were headed our way with all stops out, all lights and every siren wide open!

"I think we better get out of here," Jake said nervously.

"No! We have to face the music!" I said.

And we did. In five minutes we were surrounded by the chief of police, the fire chief, fifteen or so volunteer firemen, the head of the local Veterans association and lots of his members, the county sheriff and just about everybody else in town!

Colonel Alfred Craig, the head of the

Veterans' Club, had been in what he called "The Big War." He thought the other wars were not worth mentioning. He also thought there was a communist behind every bush, and he sure thought we Buck brothers were spies.

"Pinkos!" he snorted and held onto Joe's collar in one hand and Jake's in the other. "I been keeping an eye on these three. Commies, boys, and we caught 'em red-handed!"

A mutter went around the group, but then Chief Potter said, "Now wait a minute, Al, let the boys tell their side of it."

"Ain't no bleedin' heart liberals needed here, Potter," Craig said. "They're card-carrying commies, and that's the way it is!"

Well, I guess if he'd had his way, we'd have been shot at sunrise, but the worst thing that happened was that we all went down to the courthouse and tried to get the thing settled.

We might have, too, if the phone hadn't kept ringing off the hook.

All that steel and iron that went up in the air? Well, it had to come down *somewhere!*

The first call was from James Grady, a prissy man who mowed his yard wearing a necktie. He'd just gotten a slab poured for his drive, and the cement was all liquidy. At the time of the explosion, he'd been running a board over it to smooth it out, as he'd been doing for about three hours. Then suddenly this heavy window weight came out of the sky and landed right in the middle of his cement. He was raging mad because it ruined a necktie that his father had worn to the Democratic Convention in 1934!

The next call was a little more serious. Lots of ball bearings were in that junk that went up, and I guess most of them came down in the worst place in the world—Daily's Greenhouse! Can you imagine the sight! It must have been like someone taking target practice with a shotgun!

Then a metal statue of Venus with a clock in her belly fell right in the middle of Maud Tuttle's picnic table in her backyard. She'd been trying to get Lionel Shadwell to propose to her for five years, and she had him just about ready, when that blasted clock fell right in the middle of her freshly baked blueberry cobbler! It went off like a bomb, covering Lionel and Miss Maud up to their eyes in blueberries. But the worst was when Miss Maud saw that statue with no clothes and no arms. She just fainted and Lionel made his escape—never to return. Miss Maud was going to sue us for breach of promise, even though that didn't make sense. (The poor woman was never quite the same after that!)

Well, we stayed up all night and someone called in the National Guard and it got in the papers the next day and there was a special bulletin on the radio. The worst thing was when the Reverend Alvin Dinwiddie, the new Methodist pastor, got invaded by pigs. He was new in town, and that night he was meeting with the leaders of his church over at Si Humbolt's place, just on the edge of town.

Si had a super place, as you'd expect from a rich man. He was also the most important member of the church. His wife had fixed up a nice table full of cakes and punch, and they had just sat down. The new preacher was nice enough though timid, and his wife was worse.

When that iron came down, some of it landed right on the rump of Elizabeth, Si's prize New Hampshire sow, who must have weighed three hundred pounds. When that iron slapped her rump, she just waded through that fence made of two by sixes and went crazy with fear. If only she'd been pointed toward the woods. Instead, she was aimed at the house and went through the door without bothering to open it. *Crash!* She went sailing into Si's house, followed by three other sows about her size.

It did come as sort of a shock to Si when Elizabeth and her friends came running through the dining room. But the Reverend and Mrs. Dinwiddie were pure overwhelmed. Elizabeth tried to sit in the Reverend's lap, and when his chair broke and he hit the floor, she tried Mrs. Dinwiddie, who was constitutionally opposed to the idea. She responded to the whole thing by fainting.

It wasn't exactly the kind of supper Si had had in mind, but he said later, "A preacher had ought to be able to handle a thing like that. After all, some of our church members ain't even as polite as Elizabeth."

Well, the best thing I can say about the night the chimney blew up was that it didn't come to stay. It came to pass! But not soon enough!

FIVE
Invitation
to Disaster

All of the profit we stood to make off the Abbott's chimney went to pay for damages, and all Jake could say was "Well, I guess the ball's in your court, Barney. Now what's this big scheme of *yours?*"

I'd been so busy trying to stay out of jail over *his* nutty scheme that I hadn't had time to talk to the professor, so I put Jake off. "I don't want you messing with it, Jake," I said. "*I'll* handle it!"

He glared at me and said, "Well, I like that! After I break my back trying to cut corners on the expense, my own brother won't trust me!"

"What expense did you cut?"

"On the invitations!" he said with a satisfied grin. "I got the best deal in the western world on some invitations."

"How much?" I demanded.

"Free as air, brother mine!" He kissed his fingertips and added, "I figure we saved at least two hundred bucks. Now that's not hay, is it?"

"Well, let's see what they look like."

"Oh, they're already gone," he said. "I got Coach to give me the list Miss Jean made up, and then I conned a few girls who write neat to address the envelopes."

"But. . . ." I had the feeling that trusting Jake with wedding invitations was like trusting a monkey in a powder house.

". . . Are you *sure* they're all right? I mean, I want this done right!"

"Best card they had in stock, and Dan's Print Shop did the printing."

I still couldn't put my finger on what was wrong. "But why were they free?"

Jake gave me that smug look that said he was smarter than somebody else. "Don't worry, Barney. I made a little deal. It's OK. By three this afternoon people all over town will be getting the good word on the wedding."

I left him gloating over his triumph and ran out to see how the professor was getting along. When I got to the spot, the first thing I saw was Tiny in one end of a ditch that was over a hundred yards long and nearly two feet deep.

He waved his shovel at me as I walked up and looked down into the ditch.

"Gee, Barney!" he said with that big smile

of his. "Look at this big old ditch I made!"

"Yes, Tiny, it sure is a nice one." I stooped down and picked up a piece of bone, then asked, "What's this ditch for?"

"Oh, shoot, it's for finding stuff! The professor is real excited, I tell you!"

"Sure enough?" That sounded good to me. I was hoping to cash in on this thing fast. "Where is he?"

"He's right over there in that tent, see?"

He pointed to a green wall tent under some big sycamore trees. I said, "Well, I have to go talk to him."

"And I'll just keep digging, Barney. It sure is fun bein' an archaeologist. That's what that girl said I was."

I left him making the dirt fly and whistling "Go Tell Aunt Rhody," and when I came close to the tent, I called out, "Professor? Xanthippe?"

"Ah, it is you, Barney!" The professor looked up from a long table covered with all kinds of pottery and bones. He was so excited that his eyes glittered like diamonds behind his thick lenses. "Where have you been? We have been worried!"

I didn't really want to tell him that I'd been firing off dynamite, so I just said, "Well, I've been real busy. Looks like you're finding a lot of good stuff."

He picked up a bone, stared at it, then shook his head. "Yes, but it is confusing!"

"What do you mean?"

"Oh, everything is old. This bone is very ancient." He stared at it through a magnifying glass, then tossed it down on the table. He picked up a round object and handed it to me. "This is old also, but not nearly so old as the bone."

I couldn't help asking, "Is this stuff worth a lot, Professor?"

He stared at me as if the thought had not occurred to him. "A lot of money?"

"Well, yes."

"I suppose it is," he said slowly. "I do not think of such things. I am interested in science."

"I'll bet *you* think of money a lot, don't you?" Xanthippe had come up behind me so quietly I hadn't heard her until she spoke. She had a snobby look on her face, and I wanted to throw her in a tub of oil and watch her soften! But I didn't.

"Well, I do need some money, to be truthful." Sooner or later we were going to have to talk about money, and I wanted it to be sooner. "So you think we can make some profit on this, Professor Vandiver?"

"Oh, certainly there is a possibility. We have dug one ditch, and already there is an abundance of specimens from the past. But it does not make sense!" He reached out and touched the bone I had uncovered. There was a tag on it. He stared at it, then shook his head. "I have never seen so many different artifacts in such a small area and covering such a long span of time. It may be the most momentous discovery of modern times!"

"Papa, he's not interested in that," Xanthippe said. "He's just a greedy American."

I stared at her. "Aren't you an American?"

"Unfortunately, yes. But I have a European mind-set—a scientific approach."

"Now, daughter, there are many fine American scientists," the professor said. He shook his head and added, "But I must confess that if this is what it appears to be, it will be a discovery that will rock the world of archaeology. Here in the middle of a rural setting to find coins, weapons, jewelry—all in one dig! Why, it must have been a tremendously complex society—far beyond anything anyone has ever dreamed existed in this part of the world."

He was so excited he went back to his scraping and peering with a magnifying glass, saying, "I will have something to tell you tomorrow. Come back then. . . ."

"Actually, I was hoping—" I started to say, but Xanthippe grabbed me by the arm and jerked me out of the tent.

"Don't disturb my father when he's working," she said.

We walked over to where Tiny was still digging like a mole, and Xanthippe said sharply, "Stop being so careless, you idiot! You'll destroy the specimens!"

Tiny paused with a shocked look on his

face, his grin faded. "I–I'm really sorry, Miss Tippi—" he started to say.

"And my name is Miss *Xanthippe!*" she snapped. "I wish you had enough sense to at least get my name right."

"Yes, ma'am," Tiny said faintly. He had a shamed look on his face, and his thick shoulders sagged as he bent over the shovel.

"But he can pronounce *archaeologist* perfectly, can't you, Tiny?" I said. Then I grabbed Xanthippe by the arm and practically dragged her away.

"What–what are you doing?" she said in a shocked voice. "You let me go!"

I didn't pay a speck of attention, but when I got her away from where Tiny was digging, I whirled her around and said, "Miss Xanthippe Vandiver, if the way *I'm* saying that awful name of yours pleases you, I'm going to tell you something! You may have an IQ of ten million, but you don't have the manners of a stinking *goat!*"

She gasped, and her face turned pale as a piece of paper. "You can't talk to me that way!"

"Sure I can. I'm doing it." I was mad clear through, and I didn't care what came of it. "That *idiot*, as you call him, is one of the sweetest guys in the whole world. He's not as bright as some people, but he's never said an unkind thing to a soul! He spends most of his time helping an old couple who'd be in a nursing home if it weren't for him, and cutting wood for widows—and digging holes in the ground for ingrates with no manners! And he's not going to do it anymore! I'm going to take him back to town. Let's see you dig that trench. That scientific spirit you're so proud of ought to be a great help!"

I'd said too much. I always did when I got mad. But I started to go to Tiny, and then I heard this weird noise that sounded like a hiccup. When I turned around, there she was, her face all twisted up tight with big tears running down her cheeks.

What could I do but go and say as gently as I could, "Now, Tippi, don't cry. I just blew up. Shouldn't have said all that stuff!"

"Nooooo!" She started blubbering like a spanked baby. "I'm always doing mean–mean things like that!"

"Now, don't cry. . . ," I said, and then wouldn't you know it, she grabbed me and I had to put my arms around her to hold her up. She was so little that she seemed like a baby, but she was as old as I was.

She sobbed and sobbed and got my shirt all damp. Then finally she pulled back, and her face got all red. "Do you have a handker-chief?"

"Here. It's not too clean."

"I don't care," she said, wiping her face. "I feel sorry for Tiny, believe it or not. But you know who else I feel sorry for?"

"Who?"

"Me!" She looked up at me and pulled her

63

glasses off. Her eyes were the oddest color—a deep violet, and I noticed a few other things about her. But she didn't notice me staring at her.

"You know what my IQ is, Barney? Over 150."

"Gosh, you're a genius!"

"Yes, and do you know how much *fun* it is to be reading at the age of three? To be always light years ahead of the other kids in your class? Do you know what it's like to be so much smarter than everyone else that they hate you for it?"

I had to grin at that. "Well, actually, Tippi—You don't mind my calling you that now, do you?—I've never had the problem."

She shook her head, and that smooth raven hair shone like black silk in the sun. "You think it would be fun, but it's not. And you know what else? It makes you act awful! I know I do, but I can't quit!"

"But don't you have lots of smart friends?"

"No. I don't have any friends." That shook me up a little, and she gave a faint smile. "What boy wants a girl who's smarter than he is? Or what girl for that matter?"

"Well, *I* don't give a dead rat how smart you are."

She stared at me and her mouth was parted in wonder. "Really? You don't care?"

"That's what I said. I can do lots of things *you* can't do. Can you skin a coon? Can you do a one-and-a-half off the one meter board?

Can you whistle by sticking your fingers in your mouth?" I laughed at her expression. "Of course you can't. So why should you feel proud because you have a couple more IQ points than me?"

I was laying it on pretty thick, but I noticed that even with just a little encouragement she was perking up. "Tell you what, Tippi, I'm going to take you in hand. Manage you, so to speak. I know all the kids in this town, and I'm going to get you in with them, make you a part of the crowd."

She batted her eyelashes, which were long and thick, and asked eagerly, taking my hands in hers, "Would you really do that for me, Barney?"

"Never fear, Barney Buck is here!" I said with a smile. "Now I've got lots to do what with getting a wedding all put together—"

"You have to do what?" she asked, her eyes enormous, and of course I had to explain it all to her.

"Why, that's just *thrilling*, Barney!" she said, still holding onto my arm. "Can I help?"

"You sure can, if your father can spare you."

She rushed over to the tent right away, and by the time I had talked with Tiny long enough to get the smile back on his face, she was back.

There was a smile on her face that made her look good, and she was holding a huge glass with an iced drink. "Here, Tiny," she said with a warm glance. "I brought you some lemonade. You sit down and drink it slow. And don't work so hard, you hear me now?"

Tiny looked at her anxiously, and I guessed it was the first time she'd spoken kindly to him, and when he saw her smile, he just wiggled all over like a puppy. "Gee, thanks, Miss Tippi!"

We left and she said thoughtfully, "He's really nice, isn't he?"

"He really is. Most people are, Tippi."

She snuggled up close to me and said, "I like that name! That's what I want to be called from now on."

It sure beat Xanthippe!

All the kids hung out at Winter's Drugstore, so I took Tippi there to meet the gang.

"There they are," I said to Tippi as we went in. I led her to the back booth and said, "Hey, this is Tippi Vandiver." They all looked up, and I called their names. "Tippi, this is my brother Jake, and my younger brother Joe. This is Debra Simmons, and Helen Stone. That's Danny Bullock, Fred Simms. . . ."

I went all around, and Tippi just sort of mumbled, keeping her head down. I pulled Debra to her feet, pushed Tippi into her seat, and said, "Can I see you for just a minute, Debra?"

When I pulled her outside, I said "Debra, I would like for you to be nice to Tippi. She's a little shy, but I'm going to bring her out of it.

66

So what you need to do is just sort of include her in your hen parties, you know?"

Debra Simmons was my best friend and had been since I first came to Goober Hollow. She hadn't been all that pretty three years before, but she'd been shaping up pretty well, and she was a smart girl. In fact she could run coons better than most boys! Not better than *me*, of course! (That would've been too much!)

I've tried to keep our relationship on what they call a "platonic plane," but she'd never really dug that.

She stood there, tapping that dimple in her chin with one finger, and I knew I was in trouble. Whenever she got upset, her huge eyes lit up with something close to fire. She looked at me now like I'd just escaped from the Oklahoma Home for the Silly.

"Now let me get this straight," she said in that husky voice of hers. "You come in with a strange girl clinging to you like a leech, and you pull me outside and tell me that I am supposed to sponsor her in my . . ." She tapped her full lower lip then, seeming to hunt for the word. "My *hen party*, I think you called it?"

Well, I stepped into a number-five ought steel trap once, and as I stood there absorbing that glance of hers, I felt I'd done it again!

I started explaining real fast how it was, and I ended up saying, ". . . So you see, Debra, the kid is just too smart, in a way. I thought that you could sort of help her out. I mean, you've never been put down for being smart."

Debra stopped tapping her lip and stared at me for so long I got nervous. Finally, she shook her head and smiled. "Barney, every time I think that you have developed a little tact, you manage to convince me otherwise."

"Gee, thanks a lot, Debra!" I said with a grin. "Does that mean you'll help?"

"Yes! Now let's get inside."

We went back, and Joe was talking at a rate of fifty words a second with gusts up to a hundred. He'd found out about the archaeology bit, and anything scientific really set him off. But it was good for Tippi, because she didn't have to talk much!

Things turned out pretty good, and I gave Debra a wink about thirty minutes later. Getting close enough to whisper, I said, "I think this is going to work! See how well she's doing?"

Just then Wally Baxter came in the front door and made a bee line for me. He was grinning from ear to ear and holding some paper.

"Hey, Barney, I just picked up my invitation to the wedding! I think it's great!" Then he burst out laughing, and we all stared at him.

"Well, Wally, I'm glad it makes you so happy," I said.

"It's—it's the dangdest invitation I ever saw!" he burst out laughing again, and I pulled the invitation out of his hand.

I opened it up and read it. It was a beautiful job of printing, and the words were just right.

Wally was falling over a chair, his face flushed from laughter.

"I don't see anything funny about this invitation," I said.

"Look–look at the *back!*"

I flipped the card over, and I never wanted to drop into the earth so much in my whole life! In fact, even my face dropped.

"What is it, Barney?" Debra asked.

I showed her the back of the card.

"Oh, no!" she half-screamed, and the rest crowded around to stare.

On the back of the card was a picture of a force plunger, what some people call a plumber's friend. And over it in big bold letters was the name of a local plumber—Ray Watley's Plumbing Service. Then there was his number, and under the picture of the plunger were the words: "Stopped-up Drains Our Specialty!"

A sort of dead silence settled over the group, and even Wally shut up. Finally, I said, "Jake, I take it this is how you got the free invitations?"

"Sure! Neat, ain't it, Barney?"

I stared at him. "You don't see anything odd in having a plumber's ad on the back of the invitation?"

"No. What's odd about it?"

They say you can't make a silk purse out of a sow's ear. Well, you couldn't stop my brother from trying to save a buck.

"Barney, we have to do something!" Debra said. "Jean will just *die!*"

"Too late," I said bitterly. "They're already mailed. We can't get them back from the mailman."

"Oh, we didn't send them by mail," Jake said. "We all just put them in the boxes ourselves. Saved nearly thirty bucks in postage."

"You did!" I shouted. "Then we can get them back!"

If I ever did any organizing, it was then! I sent those kids out to go to every house where they'd delivered an invitation and had them retrieve them any way they could! "If they've taken them out of the box, ring the bell and talk them out of those dumb things! Beg, fall on your knees, threaten them with death—just get them all back!"

Well, you know it worked! We got every one of them back. Oh, a few had been opened, but everyone loved Coach and Miss Jean, so they hid their grins and promised to keep it quiet.

All worked out well, except for one thing. I was reminded that one invitation was still unclaimed—old Mrs. Larsen's. She was a gripey old woman who lived out at the edge of town. I had to go right by there to take Tippi back to the dig, so we stopped off to get it.

I was just reaching into the mailbox when I heard a door open and someone said, "I caught you! Robbing the United States Mail!"

There she stood with a shotgun pointed right at me!

It came as quite a shock to Professor Vandiver when he was confronted by Chief Potter, who had to tell him that his daughter was in the slammer charged with being an accessory to a crime—robbing the United States Mail! Of course, it didn't take long to get us out—once things were properly explained and Mrs. Larsen was calmed down enough to stop pressing charges and all.

SIX
A Tiny Part

For the first time in my life Christmas caught me off guard. Usually right after Thanksgiving I'd look forward to decorating, buying presents, and enjoying activities at church. But trying to get the wedding all planned and spending a lot of time working with the professor and Tippi at the dig had just about worn my legs off.

By now we had a small mountain of artifacts stacked in a big tent, and the professor kept shaking his head, but I could tell he was really excited about all the stuff we kept digging up.

"We must not be too quick," he said over and over. "We must be sure."

"But this is all old stuff, isn't it, Professor?" I asked him one day.

"Yes, but it is all *mixed up!* And I cannot make *anything* of this stone!"

"What kind of language is it?"

"Oh, it is the modern letters, not runes or any other ancient letters. But I cannot *read* the meaning. If we could only find the other pieces."

But we never did, although Tiny dug up enough ground to bury a house! Finally, the professor agreed to hold a press conference in a week, and when I looked at the date I was shocked to see that the date would be December 28!

I'd been so buried with work that when I surfaced, it was a shock to learn that the rest of the world was still interested in Christmas and stuff like that.

"Well!" Debra said the next day as I walked up to where she was sipping a malt at the drugstore. "Who is this stranger who has suddenly appeared from nowhere?" She looked around the room and added, "There used to be a boy named Barney Buck who was a pretty good guy. Wonder whatever happened to him?"

I wrestled her malt out of her hand and drained it, then said, "He died of doing good deeds. Are you going to eat those potato chips?"

"Yes," she said firmly and slapped my hand. "You don't deserve any—not after the way you've acted."

"Aw, cut it out, will you, Deb? I've been real busy. What's been happening?"

"All of the rest of us have been enjoying

the Christmas season. I suppose you've been spending many hours picking out presents?"

Presents! I hadn't bought a single one, but I never let on.

She was staring at me and I conned her. It's not hard to fool girls when it becomes necessary. They hear what they want to hear, not what you actually *say.* For example, every time a new mother holds her baby out for you to admire and it looks like eight pounds of hamburger meat, what do you do? Usually most of us lie.

I used to do that, until finally I decided it wasn't right. Now all I do is take a long look at the kid, sigh deeply, then point a finger at it and say as impressively as I can, *"Now there's a baby!"* All I'm doing is stating a biological fact, but what they hear me say is, "Now there's a *beautiful* baby!"

So when Debra asked if I'd bought presents and I hadn't, I tried to look as annoyed as I could and snapped at her, "Do you think I'm the kind of guy that would neglect an important thing like *that?* Why, I must have spent a week just trying to decide what to get *you!"*

I had, too—back in October. But she fell for it, and she gave me one of those world-class smiles that she always had on tap. "Oh, Barney!" she breathed and gave my arm a good squeeze.

It was like shooting fish in a barrel! Anyway, I ordered a double malt and siphoned it off while Debra chattered along, bringing me up to date on things.

". . . And I think you did the right thing about Tippi," she said, giving my ear a yank and adding, "but if I thought you really *liked* her, I'd have let her go down the drain without a tear."

"Not my type. Now you're my type, woman—earthy. A simple peasant."

"Never mind all that! But you know, Barney, Tippi's really a brain, and after she opened up to me, she told me how hard it is to be a gifted person."

"We do have our problems," I said sadly. "You plain ordinary folks just don't know!"

"How are you doing in math, you gifted person?" she said wickedly. Then when I hid my face in the malt glass, she went on. "Of course she's been real busy helping her father. But she's been to church a few times, and Tommy Powell really took to her. Took her skating out at the rink."

"Yea, but he's a brain, too," I argued.

"I know, but they went with Larry and Lena—which made a nice balance. Neither one of *them* ever set the curve!"

"Well, that's my good deed for the year." I hit bottom in the malt, and the noise rattled the windows. "Well, what else is new?"

"I'm not through telling you about Tippi, but I guess you know about her and Tiny?"

"Tiny? No, what about them?"

"You mean they didn't tell you? Well, they

both have parts in the Christmas pageant."

I stared at her. "Tiny? He has a part? You mean he's one of the shepherds who wears a bathrobe and never says anything?"

Debra sniffed. "Certainly not, you hermit!" A smile lit up her face, and she said, "Tiny plays the role of the innkeeper, the one who turns Mary and Joseph away from the inn."

"But he'll never remember his lines!"

"Oh, you just don't have any faith at all, Barney! He'll do fine, and the best part is that Tippi is playing the role of Mary."

"Hey, that's cool!"

"It's even better because she's going to coach Tiny for his part. They're onstage at the same time, and she can even whisper the lines to him if he forgets."

"Well . . ."

"Barney, it's really *good!* Tippi shared with me how she's always been real awkward around people like Tiny—'special' people. She told me she was afraid of them and was really pretty mean to them. So this is a real fine thing! You did real fine, Barney!" Then her eyes twinkled, and she said, "By the way, Tippi told me about how you bawled her out, then had to take her in your manly arms and comfort her when she broke down."

I made my voice deep. "Man does what he's gotta do, woman!"

"Maybe I ought to learn how to be little and helpless?" she said with a smile, while I cleared my throat, which always got clogged up whenever she whispered in that husky voice of hers.

"If something doesn't come out of this project to bring in a pile of money, you can comfort *me!*" I said.

"It'll work out. Tippi told me her father is really convinced that when the news breaks, there'll be all kinds of publicity—even in *Newsweek* and on TV. You'll be rich!"

"Well, like I always say, Debra, it's better to be rich, healthy, and good looking than it is to be poor, sick, and ugly!"

Our church was packed for the pageant, as usual. Mrs. Roberts, the pastor's wife, always directed it, and just about everybody in Clark County came.

Usually I was in it, but this year I was sitting in the front row with Coach and Debra. The choirs had all done their music, and we'd had a little sermonette by Brother Roberts, so now we were coming to the big production, the highlight of the evening.

"Hey, Coach, only seven more days of freedom!" I punched him in the ribs. "I bet you've been having some sad times, thinking about all the high old times you won't be having when you're an old married man!"

He grinned at me and said, "But think about how I'll never have to cut grass or go after a quart of milk at the store or carry the garbage out, Barney. I'll have free help to do all the stuff that husbands hate to do. Three strong, healthy body servants to do all the dirty work."

"You two hush!" Debra whispered fiercely. "The play is about to begin!"

"Yeah," I whispered back. "Say a prayer for Tiny, you guys!"

"He'll do fine," Debra said. "Tippi made him go over his part about ten million times. He couldn't forget his lines if he *wanted* to!"

The overhead lights dimmed. Then the music began and the play was on.

I wonder how many times it's been done— the Christmas story? As I sat there in the darkness waiting for the actors to come on, I thought about how all over the world people were seeing the story of the birth of Jesus. In white frame one-room churches, in cathedrals, in grass huts in Africa, and under the skies in the South Seas. I thought of how kids of all races were playing shepherds and Wise Men—Chinese, Eskimos, Swedes, Bantus, Mexicans—all still excited about that birth in a stable two thousand years ago. And I thought, too, that no matter how smart we get, how many computers are buzzing, or how many men we put on the moon—none of it means really anything apart from that Baby born in that barn!

Most people have probably seen the play over and over. It doesn't change much from year to year. Everyone knows we don't go to a Christmas pageant to see how it ends, but to enjoy thinking about Jesus' birth and what it means!

The guys had done a great job of staging. When the lights came up over the stage, there was the stable, straw and all. To the left was a door that had to be the inn, and the stable was visible to the right. There was lots of straw with a couple of live chickens clucking around! That was a real good touch, I thought!

The pastor's voice came over the speaker system with the words from Luke: "And it came to pass in those days, that there went out a decree from Caesar Augustus, that all the world should be taxed. . . ."

Mrs. Roberts had really done a number on the pageant this year, putting in a few extra twists. She had a couple of Roman soldiers appear off to one side with a spot over them. They were talking about the tax and how hard it would be for people to travel to their own city just to pay it.

Then over on the other side a spot came on, and there were Mary and Joseph talking about how dangerous it would be to make the journey to Jerusalem with the baby about to be born.

Thad Russell was Joseph, and he was really good, but Tippi was out of sight! She was so small and looked so fragile in her costume. Debra had seen the rehearsal. "I think Tippi has a natural gift for drama,

Barney," she'd said. "She just *becomes* Mary in the play!"

Usually, the shepherds and the Wise Men come down the aisles and the rest of the action is on stage, but this time it was different. Mrs. Roberts had really tried to get a cross section of the whole period with people all over the auditorium doing their parts. It seemed confusing at first, but after we got used to it, we really got caught up in the *drama* of the thing!

It's the same way with a *great* book or movie—you just forget where you are you get so involved. That's what happened that night. The whole congregation sort of *joined in* and became a part of the old story!

As the action unfolded, I found myself leaning forward, clenching my fists and gritting my teeth. It was that tense.

Everybody was on the edge of their seats as Joseph and Mary came down one of the aisles, outlined by a blue spotlight that followed them all the way down to the stage. They stopped once and Joseph made her rest and they talked about God taking care of them.

"But we must find a place *soon*, Joseph!" Mary said, and she managed to get the idea across so strongly that we were all pulling for her with all our might.

Then they went on slowly toward the stage, and Joseph said, "Look, Mary. There's an inn! Surely we can get a room for you!"

So they went up to the door and Joseph knocked on it softly, then louder when there was no answer.

Then the door opened and there was the innkeeper. Tiny Pringle looked the part. He was big and he'd let his beard grow for a couple of weeks, so he didn't look at all like your usual innkeeper in a church play!

He didn't *sound* like one either, because when he said, "What do you want?" he nearly rattled the rafters! Tiny always spoke so softly that that rough baritone caught me off guard. Besides that, he looked *rough!* Tiny always had a smile on his face and was always anxious to please folks, but you forgot that when this rough, hard-talking guy stood framed in the doorway with his arms across his chest, glaring down at the couple in front of him.

"We—we need a room for the night," Joseph said.

"You want a room, do you?" Tiny boomed and managed to put a cruel snarl in his voice. "You got as much chance of getting a room in this inn as I have of finding gold in my soup!"

Tiny pushed his way out of the door and came to tower over the couple. He glared down at them, and it was an exceptionally good glare. I don't know how they'd taught him to act, but he was really *into* the role.

"It wouldn't have to be anything very elaborate. . . ," Joseph said, but Tiny just threw his head back and roared with laughter.

"Do you know how many Jews there are in this town come to pay their tax? Why, the whole place is crawling with them, like fleas on a dog!"

"But, just a small room, in the loft, just anything!" Joseph pleaded.

The innkeeper just swelled up with anger at that. "You fool, they're stacked up like cordwood in my place already! I have to step over them to get to my own bed!"

He really ranted and raved, and Mary and Joseph just seemed to shrink down, as if they were worn out.

Then when Tiny finished and went back to the door, he stepped inside and said, "I can't help you. Should have had better sense than to come at a time like this. On your way!"

I got so caught up in the thing I actually wanted to punch Tiny out! Well, the innkeeper in him anyway.

Then Mary said, "Please, can I speak with you?"

"It's late, woman!" Tiny growled.

"Yes, but just a word. . . ," Mary said softly. Then she began telling the innkeeper that they had come so far; and she told him that it wasn't just a matter of the tax, but God was going to do a great work among the people of the land!

Tiny stood there, arms locked over his chest, and there was a hard look on his face. He kept shaking his head stubbornly, saying, "There's no room, I tell you!"

But Mary kept on speaking, and Tippi really got everybody in the audience uptight! She was so small, and there was a plea in her voice as she stood there. The spot was right on her upturned face. She looked so. . . . Well, I don't know what, but it was hard to look at her and not think of the real Mary as she might have come to the real inn.

Then Tippi went up closer to Tiny, and she put her hand on his arm, saying, "I know you don't have much room, but I'm so very tired and. . . ." She seemed to flinch, then said in a whisper that barely carried, "I–I don't have much time!"

There was a dead silence in the church. It gripped all of us—how bad it must have been when it had really happened. Tippi made us see the terrible need for help that the real Mary and Joseph had had, and I guess all of us were just about sick when we realized that they were going to be turned away into the dark and the cold.

Tiny was looking down at her, and his face was strange. He still looked tough as leather, looking down at Tippi. But there was a troubled light in his face, I could tell.

He seemed to stumble over his next line: "I–I tell you, there's no room." His voice wasn't nearly so loud, and I thought he must be having trouble remembering his lines.

Mary put her hand on his arms again, looked up into his face, and said, "Please, help me!"

Then Tiny's face broke into pieces!

His lips started quivering, his chin wobbled, and he batted his eyes like he had something in them. He was weaving a little, too, from side to side, and I thought he was going to be sick.

Mary said one more time, "Please, won't you let us come in?"

Two huge tears rolled down Tiny Pringle's cheeks. Then he swallowed, nodded, and said in a big voice, "Sure you can! You just come on in, Miss Mary! I'll take care of you!"

Did you ever see a movie when they *froze* the action? Everything was moving along at a fast pace, and then they just stopped and made a single picture out of it?

Well, that's what happened at the moment that Tiny said his line. Tippi's jaw dropped and she just stood dead still and there was an awful blank look on her face. If Tiny had just forgotten his line, she could have cued him, but she was so stunned that she couldn't think of her own line—which wouldn't have fit into Tiny's new concept of the story anyway!

Then Tiny just stepped forward and put his big arms around Joseph and Mary, and the biggest smile I ever saw came through his tears as he said, "Yawl just come on in and set!" in the best Arkansas dialect ever used in the Christmas pageant. Then he pulled them into the inn, telling them how he'd put down a pallet for them to sleep on.

Then he slammed the door, and there it was. The stage was empty and bare. I'm sure Mrs. Roberts had fainted dead away. There was no way in the world to turn the thing around.

Then you know what happened?

The whole audience got up and began clapping and shouting like mad! Tiny Pringle may have padded his part a little, but we loved it!

We were all laughing and crying at the same time, and I guess it pretty well showed that what this world needs are people like Tiny who think more of loving people than of reading the right line!

SEVEN
All the King's Horses

After the pageant, Tiny's reputation was made for all time. People who'd never had a good word for him stopped him on the street and told him how much they'd enjoyed watching him do the play. If it had been me, I'd have swollen up with pride like a poisoned pup, but Tiny just ducked his head and grinned.

The only one who didn't love the play was Tippi. She got it into her head that Tiny had made a fool out of her. I tried to tell her that everybody loved the way it came out, but Tippi had that kind of stubbornness you meet now and then. She had had it in her mind exactly how the play should have gone, and never mind that it turned out *better* another way.

She had been doing so well, learning to get along with the gang and being in the church play. But after the play it was as though she just said, "Stop the world. I want to get off."

I was at the dig most of the time helping the professor get the exhibit ready for the press conference, which was set for the afternoon of the twenty-eighth. Tippi worked, too, but when I tried to get her to talk, she said, "Leave me alone, Barney Buck! You've made me look like a fool in front of the whole county. Isn't that enough for you?"

She froze Tiny out, too, and that just about broke the big guy's heart! He kept trying to be nice to her, but she kept shoving his face in the dirt and cutting him down all the time.

Debra was helping me on the morning of the twenty-eighth when all of a sudden she locked horns with Tippi. She'd overheard Tippi call Tiny a "big dumb ox," and then pitched into her so hard I practically had to sit on her to stop a massacre.

Tippi was red in the face, but she was too stubborn and mad to back down. She glared at both of us and said, "I'll be glad when this is over and I can get away from you hillbillies!"

Debra opened her mouth, but I pulled her away. "Let her alone, Debra. She's all mixed up."

"I'd like to have her put to sleep!" Debra said. Since she nursed sick sparrows back to health, that was all talk and we both knew it.

"I guess Tippi'll be happier when she gets back to her books and experiments," I said, but I knew she wouldn't.

Anyway, the press conference, set for two o'clock in the afternoon, turned out to be quite a happening! The professor had a fine reputation, so when the newspapers got the word that right in Arkansas we might have a find that would set the world on its ear, it drew reporters as honey draws flies.

There was John Starr from the *Arkansas Democrat*, Robert McCord from the *Arkansas Gazette*, all the commentators from the TV stations, not to mention representatives from the colleges and universities all over the state, and even a few from Texas and Louisiana!

Cars and pickups were jammed together as if it was a Razorback football game. There were microphones so thick you couldn't spit without hitting one!

All the dignitaries were on a little platform that had been set up, and the governor was there with his wife and just about everybody who was anybody.

Dr. McBeth, president of the college in Conway, finally got the ball rolling. He settled everybody down, then gave a speech about how fortunate we were to have a man like Professor Vandiver in our state. He listed all the degrees the professor had and all the things he'd done, and that took a long time.

Tippi was standing by her father and beaming with pride. That was good. If she couldn't get along with kids her own age, I guessed it was a good thing she had a father to admire.

It was election year, so the governor had to get his oar in. (Every time a kitten got stuck up in a tree you'd see his picture on the front page of the papers getting it down. Then his opponent had to have equal time, so it went on and on.)

Finally, Professor Vandiver got to address the crowd, and he looked tired. He'd been working night and day, and I knew he thought it was too soon to announce the find, but I'd nagged him into it so we could get into the money.

"My friends," he said solemnly, "we live in a time that is almost solely concerned with the present. Either men are seeking to gratify a present desire, or they are laying up treasures in order to provide for an uncertain future. As a scientist and as a humanist, I feel that if we are to realize the potential that lies within our race, we must look to the past." He had a very dreamy look on his face, and Tippi moved closer to him.

He went on for a little while about how we must profit from the mistakes of the past if we were to have a good future. Then finally he got down to the business at hand.

"I have asked you to come here this afternoon, because I feel that the earth has offered us another golden nugget! Here in this isolated spot. . . ." He waved his hand around at the trees and the sky . . . "It would be easy to think that it has always been as you see it now. But this is not so! Here in this place, we have found evidence that once there was a thriving culture, one far more advanced than anyone has ever dreamed!"

He told them about all the relics we'd found, holding up a few to illustrate his discoveries, and finally he asked for questions from the audience.

"Professor, are you saying that the Indians had a more advanced culture than we've been led to believe?" a reporter from Dallas asked.

"No! What we have here is a culture much older than I would have thought possible."

John Starr of the *Democrat* asked, "You mean some sort of forgotten civilization—like Atlantis?"

The professor looked nervous, then said, "I think so. We have found coins from pre-Roman times, and we have found fossils that go back beyond written history. We have unearthed tools that are the equal of any in Europe during the early historical periods. I will show you pottery that looks so much like Greek pottery it is amazing!"

"So it's going to be a real big thing for our state?" the governor asked.

"No, not for this state!" Professor Vandiver snapped back. "It will be a great thing for the world, and that is what science should do, Governor—benefit the world!"

There was a lot of applause over that, but it was pretty clear that a lot of folks were excited about how the buried city would put Arkansas on the map.

They kept shooting questions at him,
especially a man with a beard who seemed
angry about the whole thing for some reason.

"I don't think you've been professional
about this dig, Vandiver!" he said loudly. "You
had the obligation to call other scientists in
before you made a Roman holiday out of it
with the press!"

"You may be right to some degree, Professor
Neely, but we have only a limited time to
develop the find. . . ," the professor said. I
found out later that Neely was from another
university and green with jealousy over
everything Professor Vandiver did. Neely kept
on picking at everything, and even though
Professor Vandiver tried to ignore him, I
could see he was disturbed.

Finally, he held up the stone that I had
found and said, "I offer this as one of the
mysteries that we have uncovered. It is clear
enough so far as the letters are concerned.
Obviously it is some form of Latin. . . ."
He read the inscription with a funny pro-
nunciation,

T E R S O
O L I D
S E U M A
M P O R I U

" 'Terso olid seuma mporiu.' " He shook his head and added, "We have not been able to locate the missing pieces of the stone, and I cannot find the key to this strange form of language."

Well, right then there was a disturbance, and I heard somebody calling the professor's name.

"Professor! Professor!" The crowd parted, and who was right there heading straight for the stage but Tiny!

He had something in each hand, and his face was beaming. He came to stand right in front of the stage, pride rippling in every part of his body as he spoke to the professor. The cameras were rolling, and they got him in full face.

"Professor, you done so much for me, letting me work for you and all, that I wanted to give you something."

Professor Vandiver looked embarrassed, and he started to say, "Well, that's very nice, Tiny, but. . . ."

"Oh, it's not just a necktie or something like that," Tiny said, nodding his head vigorously. "It's something you want more than anything in the world!"

Professor Vandiver stared at him, and then in an excited voice he cried out, "Tiny! Did you find the other pieces of the stone?"

"I sure enough did!" Tiny yelled at the top of his lungs. "I been digging every day and most of the nights, too! And last night I came upon 'em, and here they are!"

He handed the two pieces of the stone to the professor, who took them as if they were two diamonds. The whole crowd kind of leaned forward trying to see, and Professor Neely shoved his way up on the stage. "Put them together, Vandiver. I am the most competent Latin scholar in this country!"

The man wasn't broken out with modesty, but I guess Professor Vandiver saw he had to do it. Tippi had scooted over to the table where the finds were laid out and she was back in a flash. She put the large stone down, and very carefully her father put the two pieces into place. I leaned over and saw the entire stone all put together. Then I thought I'd fall down and die! What I saw was this:

PATTERSONS CONSOLIDATED MUSEUM AND EMPORIUM

"Patterson's Consolidated Museum and Emporium!" Professor Neely read the thing out loud. He stared at Professor Vandiver and sneered, "Is *this* the mysterious stone you've built your fantasy on, Vandiver?"

"I–I don't . . . know what. . . ." Professor Vandiver looked like he'd been kicked right in the stomach.

"Get a shot of that, boys!" one of the reporters shouted, and a hubbub broke out, everybody trying to talk at once.

Tippi's face was white as paste! If any girl had ever put all her love into one person, she was the one, and now that was breaking up right in front of her!

Finally, the professor pulled himself together. He grabbed the microphone and said, "Please! Let me have your attention!" He waited for them to quiet down, then said in a small voice, "I–I have been mistaken about this stone. Professor Neely is right. I should not have been so hasty."

I wanted to tell the crowd it was all my fault, but it wouldn't have done any good. I looked around and noticed that most of the crowd seemed to be mad at something. Then I realized that they thought Professor Vandiver had been trying to pull a fast one—in fact, trying to fool them!

They interrupted his apology, and one of them asked, "You salted this mine, didn't you, Professor?"

"Salted the mine?" Professor Vandiver asked, shaking his head. "I do not understand."

"He means you planted these things," Neely said with a grin. "Looks like you rigged the whole thing, Vandiver."

"No!" Tippi grabbed her father's arm and said, "He would not do a thing like that."

"I guess we have to believe what we see," Neely said. "Of course there have been hoaxes in the past, lots of them. But I'm shocked that a man like you would try to do such a thing, Vandiver!"

"Wait a minute!"

I looked up, and there was Uncle Dave Simmons, Debra's grandfather, pushing his way through the crowd.

Uncle Dave was in his eighties, but he was straight as an arrow, and I knew from firsthand experience he could walk most men into the ground!

He had silver hair and a face tanned like rich leather. His eyes were brown and sharp as daggers. Now he held up his hand for quiet and said, "I think you fellers better hold your horses."

"What you mean, Uncle Dave?" Charlie Peters shouted. "He's guilty as sin."

"You ought to be quite an authority on sin, Charlie, with that still you operate over at Joan."

Peters disappeared like he'd been atomized, and there was a loud laugh from the local people who knew him.

"Before you get on with crucifying the professor," Uncle Dave said, "I ought to tell you something." He looked at the reporters, and most of them must have felt they were looking down a rifle barrel. That was how sharp his eyes were.

"I came to this country in 1905, in the back of a spring wagon. Grew up in the Ouachita River bottoms. Spent my whole life in Clark County. . . ."

He got a distant look in his eye, and his voice got a little softer as he went on: "Most of the folks I knew in those days are gone now. Almost all of them. And one that I thought a heap of was J. Millington Patterson!"

"Did he have a museum, Uncle Dave?" I shouted out loud, not able to keep still.

"He sure did, Barney," Uncle Dave said with a nod. "Right here on this site." He rubbed his chin and shook his head. "I was just a boy, then, and I'd almost forgotten this place."

"Who was he, Grandpa?" Debra asked.

"Well, he was almost one of your ancestors, girl," Uncle Dave said, giving her a grin. "I was so in love with his oldest girl Elmus, I done fool things like buying flowers and writin' poetry, but she up and married Ronald Stevens."

"But what did he have here at this spot?" Professor Vandiver asked.

"Patterson made a lot of money in cotton, but he always wanted to be just what you are, Professor. Wanted to go to Egypt and places like that to dig up things. But he had a big family, so that was out. What he did was buy everything he could that other folks dug up."

"A collector?" I asked.

"That's right. He built a huge barn and filled it with all sorts of stuff. Some of it I guess you've been finding around here."

"What happened to the museum?" I asked.

"Burned to the ground in the fall of 1918, the year I went to France." Uncle Dave shook his head. "I was gone, but they told me that Patterson mourned himself into a grave over that fire. Loved that stuff he'd collected so much, I guess. Then the forestry service put out pines, and I guess everything got covered up."

Our governor always said, "My mama didn't raise no dummies!" When he saw a way to get out of the possible bad press, he jumped on it like a duck on a Junebug. "I think it's safe to say that although this find is not as old as the Professor hoped, the artifacts are still valuable? Is that correct?"

Professor Vandiver raised his head and said, "Oh, yes, they are not consistent, but there are many fine things which are quite interesting." Then he said, "I am not feeling well, so will you excuse me."

Tippi was there to grab his arm, and I felt sad to see them leave, clinging to one another. I knew that the professor thought he had ruined his career, and I knew that Tippi would just about die.

I might have died, too, for it suddenly dawned on me that there wasn't going to be any money to pay for the wedding. As far as I could see, Humpty Dumpty had been broken into a million pieces, and all the king's horses and all the king's men weren't going to put him together again!

EIGHT
Uphill
from Here

"We've got three days until the wedding, and as far as I can see, the only thing we got is a pound of rice to throw."

The three of us were slumped in the living room the morning after the press conference, and Jake had pretty well summed up the situation. He had a bleak look on his dark face, and I knew when Jake was down, things were in bad shape.

"We can do it," Joe said, nodding hopefully as he went on. "I have lots of ideas about stuff we can do. Matter of fact, I've already been working on some of them."

"What kind of *stuff* do you mean?" I asked.

"Oh, different things to make the service more impressive. Seems like every wedding I've ever been to was just like all the rest. Well, I've been working with Mr. McCoy, and we've come up with some great stuff!"

Mr. McCoy was the church custodian, and he liked Joe a lot. "I don't know how you can change a wedding service up much," I said.

"Maybe we could have the bride come down the aisle backward," Jake muttered glumly. "Now wouldn't that be different?"

"Aw, don't be silly, Jake," Joe said. "Mr. McCoy and I have been working on some ideas about lighting—even a new twist on the sound system."

"Yeah, well, you do that Joe," I said as I got up to leave. "But don't spend any money— because we don't have any. Jake, did you cancel the orders for the tuxedos?"

Jake nodded and even had a smile. "Sure, but I think we got *that* problem solved anyway. I'm working on a deal. Have to wait and see, but it looks like we can get the tuxes from an outfit in Little Rock at a special rate—practically free."

"That would be a help."

"And I've been talking to Mrs. Loman at the flower shop, Barney," Joe piped up. "We're going to be able to get a good deal. I'm going to do some wiring for her in exchange for some flowers. I'll take care of that."

"Well, we'll all have to do what we can." I went to the door, then turned and shook my head. "The biggest problem is the money for the honeymoon. Biloxi is out. I sure wish you hadn't made *that* promise, Jake!"

"Well, I like that!" Jake said indignantly.

"All I wanted was for the folks to have a great honeymoon!"

"Yeah, but what are we gonna do *now?*"

A shifty look swept across Jake's face, and he said, "Oh, well, maybe something will turn up."

I stared at him. "Jake, before you actually *do* anything, I want to know about it."

He tried to look innocent, but Jake wasn't cut out for looking innocent. "In other words, you don't trust me!"

"Not in other words, Jake, in *those* words. I don't trust you. I don't want you signing up Coach and Miss Jean for a trip to the North Pole or some nutty thing like that."

He huffed and puffed, but I went on and got into the truck. Snow was in the clouds over to the north, and I thought we'd have a white New Year's for sure.

I thought about praying for a blizzard. If that happened, nobody would be able to come to the wedding, and that was just about my best hope. But I didn't, because deep down I was sure that no matter how bad things looked, somehow we'd pull it off.

I ran around all morning lining up things, juggling with less than a third of the little money we already had. When I went into Arby's for something to eat at noon, I ran into Coach.

"Hi, Coach," I said, plumping down next to him with my food.

"Hello, Barney." He'd been out at the house

101

working, but he looked neat even in his jeans and old leather jacket. "Things going all right?" he asked.

"Oh, sure. Everything's swell!"

He took a bite of his ham and cheese, then said offhandedly, "I know these weddings always cost more than you think they will. Why don't you let me help a little?"

"No, you take care of the house and we'll take care of the rest." That was a leap of faith! And I had an idea he knew what a struggle we were having.

But he just gave me that big smile of his and said, "OK. The house is ready, and Jean comes in tomorrow. We're on our way, son."

It sounded so good to hear him call me "son" that I turned red. Usually I didn't like to talk much about stuff that I really *cared* about. That's why I had such a hard time giving a testimony in church. I always envied those people who could just let it all hang out!

But I hadn't really had much time alone with Coach for a long time, and I wanted to let him know how I felt. I cleared my throat and stared down at the food on my plate. "Coach, I–I've got something to say, and it's a little bit hard."

"Tell it like it is, son. That's the way I want the two of us to be from now on. Just plain honest."

"Well, what I want to say is, I know what a big thing it is for you and Miss Jean to take on the three of us. It would be so easy if you could just start your marriage with the two of you, then have a baby after a while." I risked a glance at him, and he was just listening with a calm look on his face. "Well, all three of us know how much you're giving up for us, so what I want to say is, we appreciate it and we all three want to be the best sons anybody ever had."

"You will be," he said.

Then I cleared my throat and went on, but it was hard. "And–and I want to say . . . I mean, what I *really* want to say is I've always wanted to say it, and couldn't but now I want to." I took a deep breath and looked up to meet his warm brown eyes. "I love you, Dale Littlejohn!"

Why was it so hard to say that? I almost strangled getting it out and my face was red as a fire engine and my heart was beating like I'd run the 440. I guess maybe it's hard to just come right out and look somebody in the eye and say, "I love you." We're setting ourselves up for rejection. What if they say, "Oh, really? Well, that's nice."

Or maybe with guys it's not the best way to keep the old macho image in good shape. I don't know, but I do know that when Coach Littlejohn smiled at me, put his arm across my shoulder, and said in that easy natural way of his, "I love you, too, Barney," I just about melted!

Ever since Dad died, no man had ever put his arm around me and told me he loved me, and it just made me feel all mushy. I already *knew* Coach loved me, but I needed to hear it *said!*

He could tell what a bad time I was having, so he said, "It's OK to cry. I do it myself sometimes."

If a real man like him could admit that, I guess that made it all right. We sat there not saying much, and then he gave me a pop on the arm and said, "See you later, son."

I finished my sandwich and headed out to the dig to get some tools I'd left. It was starting to snow, not flakes, but fine particles that burned on my face, but it was going to get serious by night.

The roads were already glazed, so I drove with a little extra care. I didn't want to get stuck or run out of gas. That was for turkeys who didn't have any judgment.

It was a good thing I went, because most of the tools hadn't been put under the tent, and they would've been buried by morning. I found all of them and took them to the tent to clean them up and coat them with a little oil so they wouldn't rust.

By the time I finished, snow was coming in big flakes. The ground was covered, and the pickup slid sideways as I left the site and headed back home. I spent a couple of hours doing the chores, thinking all the time about ways to make do for the wedding.

The phone rang as I was pulling a cherry pie together. "Hello?"

"Barney!" Professor Vandiver's voice was pitched real high, and he sounded scared. "Have you seen Xanthippe?"

"Tippi? Why, no, Professor, not since yesterday."

"I am so *worried*, Barney! We went out to the site this morning, and when I had to go back to Conway, she said she wanted to stay and work. I got back just a few minutes ago, and she was not there! I was hoping maybe you brought her into town."

"I was out there earlier, but I didn't see her. Maybe she got a ride with somebody else."

"I don't think so." His voice got lower and he said, "She has been very unhappy since the press conference, you know?"

"Sure, she took it hard, but it wasn't your fault, Professor."

"Some of it was," he said, "but I am worried about Xanthippe. She takes things too seriously. But where can she *be*?"

"I'll get right out there, Professor. Where are you now?"

"I'm calling from a little store on the highway—Wills Grocery, I believe."

"You stay put. I'll be there in a few minutes."

I called Debra and told her to tell Uncle Dave so he could get a party organized to hunt the woods. Then I was off.

Tim jumped onto the front seat, and we

headed toward the store. I was wishing I'd put chains on, but we made it without getting off into a ditch.

Snow was coming down so thick I almost missed the store, but I saw the professor standing by the road waving at me. I rolled the window down and said, "Professor, you stay here and wait for the search party. They'll be here in less than half an hour. I'm going to take Tim and see if we can find her. It's getting dark, and I don't like to think about her being in this stuff at night."

I took off and made my way to the site, then parked the truck. Tim and I took off toward the west. I had my wheat light and plenty of batteries and some stuff I might need in a backpack.

The snow was now a couple of inches deep, and I didn't really have any idea which way Tippi might have gone. Maybe I was headed directly away from her, but I had one clue— she'd always liked a little bluff that was close to a creek about three miles from the site. I'd taken her there, and she'd brought her camera and taken a picture of it. She'd gone there at least once by herself, so I thought she might have headed that way.

I said, "Sound off, Tim!" He gave me a look and then let go with that deep-chested cry that made him such a great coon dog. He knew more about coons than I did, and I guess he thought I was crazy hunting coons when they were all holed up, but he took off anyway.

If we get within a mile of her, she ought to hear Tim, I thought, and that was my only hope. I'd hunted all over these woods, and I thought I knew them pretty well, but it all looked completely different now. Everything was blanketed in soft snow, and in the dark I'd be as lost as she probably was.

I made the trip to the bluff on the run and was pretty winded when we got there. Holding my aching side, I called her name as loudly as I could, "Tippi! Tippi! Where are you?"

I listened but heard nothing. I thought of that line in Frost's poem that read: "The only other sound's the sweep of easy wind and downy flake."

There was a hissing on the ground as the wind began to whip up the flakes in small flurries like miniature whirlwinds, and the temperature was dropping fast. My hands and face were numb, and I didn't like to think about what Tippi was feeling.

Maybe she took off and followed the creek, I thought. *But which way?* I started to head east, then stopped. If she went west, I'd miss her for sure! Tim came up whining as I was trying to decide. Times like that are really gross. No time to think about it, you have to choose right off, and you can't make a mistake.

I couldn't help thinking, *Tippi may die if I take the wrong fork!* I stood there feeling helpless, and then I knew I had to make a choice. I looked up into the grey sky swarming with millions of flakes, and I prayed out loud, "Lord, show me which way to go!"

Nothing but the wind. No word from heaven at all.

Then out of nowhere my favorite line of poetry came to me. It was from one of Robert Frost's poems, "The Road Not Taken," about someone who came to a fork in the road and couldn't decide which way to go. The line was "I took the road less travelled by, and that has made all the difference."

Well, the land on the west of the creek was smooth and easy. It was the way I'd go if I wanted an easy walk. The other way was really rough, through a swampy bottom and thick with sharp hawthorn briars.

Well, I guess that's the road less travelled by, I thought. Then I hollered, "This way, Tim!" and off we went.

It was rough going! No joke. My feet were wet right away as I hit a hidden hole filled with ice water, and it wasn't long before my face was lined with scratches from the briars and vines. I kept calling her name, and Tim was howling with all his might.

We went crashing through a branch creek, breaking the skim of ice, and I nearly died from the shock of that freezing water. Then I heard Tim making a different noise. He stopped bellying like when he's on a trail and started a shrill barking the way he did when he treed a coon.

"That's no coon!" I shouted, heading toward where he seemed to be. "Tippi! Tippi! Where are you?"

I found them a hundred yards away. She was hunkered down in the base of a big hackberry tree, and Tim was licking her face. When she saw me, she got up and threw herself at me, crying, "Barney! Barney! I knew you'd come! I knew it!"

"Are you all right?" I asked when I got loose and held her out to look into her face.

"I was so scared, Barney!" She shivered in the cold and clung to me again. "I thought I was going to die!"

"Let's get out of here. Are you wet?"

"Y–yes!" She was shaking and added through clenched teeth, "I fell right into the creek!"

That was bad news! She could freeze to death if she was wet clear through. I tried to think, and finally it came to me. "There's an old deer stand right down the creek. It's got a cabin with an old wood heater. We have to get you dried out quick!"

I had to practically drag her through the woods, and it was a good thing the cabin wasn't over a quarter of a mile away. It was right beside the creek or I'd never have found it, and by some minor miracle there was dry wood for a fire!

I got a fire going and said, "I'll go outside while you get out of those wet clothes. Wrap up in this blanket and holler when you're ready."

I went outside and it was dark as pitch. I wasn't sure if we could find our way back in the dark, and if we got lost in the bottoms both of us might freeze. She called out, and I went back inside.

"Oh, the fire is so nice, Barney!" she said. I'd lit the coal oil lamp, and she was all wrapped up in the blanket I'd brought and was practically hugging the stove.

"Wring out these clothes and put them on this chair to dry," I said. I pulled a stainless steel thermos out of my pack and opened it up. As I was pouring a cup of scalding chocolate, I didn't think anything ever smelled better. "Drink some of this. Don't scald yourself. It's hot!"

She got some of it down, and her cheeks began to get red from the warmth of the stove. "Aren't you going to dry your clothes?"

"Just my socks."

She sat there sipping the cocoa as I peeled off my socks and put them on the chair close to the stove, which was beginning to glow a nice cherry red.

"Barney?"

"Yeah?"

"How'd you ever find me?"

"Your dad called me when he came back and found you gone."

"I don't mean that," she said. Her violet eyes were really enormous in her small white face. "I mean, how'd you know exactly where to come and look? I was all turned around and these woods are so big!"

"Well. . . ." I took a swallow of the cocoa, wondering whether or not to tell her about how I'd taken the road "less travelled by." I always had problems with people who said, "God told me to do this!" Not that it couldn't happen, but with me it was never that simple. Finally, I said, "Well, I just asked the Lord to guide me to you, Tippi, and he did."

She was very still, and in the golden light of the lamp her skin looked like smooth ivory. I knew she didn't know what to make of that, but she finally said, "You know what? I think that's real neat!"

Well, I'd have to have been a regular *backslider* not to have talked to her about trusting Jesus Christ after she said that! So we talked and talked that night as her clothes dried. I'd brought some sandwiches and we ate and drank the cocoa and it was all right.

Finally, she said, "But I've been such a holy terror, Barney. You don't know! I've always been smart, and that works in things besides books!"

"What do you mean?"

"Well, I learned how to—to manipulate

people when I was just a baby. I mean, I could make my parents do anything I wanted them to, and just about everybody else!" Then she dimpled up and gave me a real smile. "Not *you, of course!*"

I snorted. "I'm the world's easiest guy to manipulate, Tippi, but anyway, being a Christian doesn't mean you get a one-shot cure for all your personality problems."

"No?"

"Why, no. God forgives you for all your sins, but then what? You don't sit around in a robe and a crown waiting to die. You have to go on *being* the Christian you *become.* See? Just like a baby has to *become* a grown person, and that means falling down sometimes and getting all skinned up."

"But I'm afraid I can't do it, Barney! I'd like to, but what's going to stop me from . . . being rotten to Tiny again like I did before?"

"Tippi, even I haven't *arrived* yet! From the time you get saved and start following Christ, it's an uphill road all the way. He never promised anyone a bed of roses. But the Bible says that there are some fruits that start popping out in anyone's life who'll let Christ come in and take over their whole life."

"Fruits?"

"Sure," I said. "The fruit of the Spirit is love, joy, peace, longsuffering, gentleness, goodness, faith, meekness, temperance."

She thought about that, and finally she

said, "I can have all that if I become a Christian?"

I grinned at her. "Goes with the territory."

Xanthippe Vandiver nodded slowly and said, "I want to be a Christian then. . . ."

Finally, we managed to get some sleep, but morning came fast. Since my socks and her clothes were dried off, we got dressed and headed for my house. All the way back, we talked about what it means to be a Christian. Exciting stuff!

NINE
Countdown to
a Wedding

Tippi called her father to let him know she
was safe, and I called Uncle Dave to say the
same thing. Then we ate and went around the
house to do a little final cleaning. I looked at
Tippi standing by the kitchen door. She was
wearing old jeans and a plaid red shirt that
came nearly to her knees.

I grinned at her, thinking how she'd lit up
like a light bulb ever since she had "hit the
glory trail," as Uncle Dave described it when
someone accepts Jesus.

"Barney," she said, "I want to do something
to help with the wedding!"

"Well, the wedding is day after tomorrow
and practically nothing's done. Take your best
shot."

"How about the rehearsal dinner tomorrow
night?"

"Jake said he'd come up with something—which is probably what General Custer said just before he left for Little Big Horn!"

"How about the wedding cake and the refreshments for the reception?"

"Hey, can you make a cake? I'll love you forever if you'll take care of that job!"

Tippi got red and started to say something, but just then I heard something and turned to the window. "There they are! Come on, Tippi!"

We ran out to the front porch, and a blue Ford Blazer shot out of the woods, roared down the road, and skidded to a stop just before going into our living room. I think a stock car driver must have taught Coach how to drive!

He'd gone to Little Rock to pick Jean up, and the two of them came piling out of the Blazer followed by a young woman with blonde hair. She looked so much like Miss Jean that she had to be her sister.

Then Jake, Joe, Tiny, Debra, and about six other kids who'd been helping with the church and other stuff scrambled out. There was a lot of chattering. Then everybody got quiet as Miss Jean got her first look at her wedding present—the house all fixed up like new.

The snow made a nice backdrop, and the big catalpa trees were so loaded with snow that they seemed to be leaning down and hugging the house.

Her eyes got big as pizza plates when she

saw it. "Oh, Dale! It looks like a Currier and Ives print!" she whispered.

Coach had really done a number on the old place. He'd put on white siding, and a blue roof with shutters to match. The old chimney was cleaned and painted, and the old fence had been knocked down and replaced with a new wrought iron one around the house.

She didn't have time to look long, because Coach pulled her inside, and we all crowded around as he proudly showed her the new ceilings, white as the snow outside, and all the wallpaper and the new rugs, thick and cinnamon-colored. She went into spasms over the gleaming new oak cabinets in the kitchen, in fact over everything.

When we finally wound up in the living room, she threw her arms around him and squealed, "Dale, it's the very best wedding present any girl ever got!" Then she gave him a big kiss, and I will have to say he didn't resist too strenuously!

All the kids were hollering, and Jake kissed the back of his hand with a big smacking noise, yelling, "Watch it there, you guys. There are innocent children present!"

Coach pried himself loose and said, "Oh, my goodness. My manners are slipping. Barney, this is Ellen, Jean's sister. She came all the way from Boston to be Jean's maid of honor."

"Hi, Ellen." I put out my hand, and she

looked at it for what seemed like a long time. Then she gave me a limp shake and nodded. "Glad to have you in the family."

"Thank you." She spoke in a neutral voice, and there was a funny look on her face as if maybe she smelled something bad and didn't want to mention it. *Maybe that's the way people from Boston look,* I thought. She was taller than Miss Jean, and maybe five years older. She was wearing funny clothes, the kind you see either at yard sales or on the pages of women's fashion magazines.

"This is Tippi," I said, and when Ellen looked at the worn jeans and the ratty old shirt Tippi had on, her eyes sort of glazed over. I saw her nose go up in the air just a fraction. Then she mumbled, "Pleased, I'm sure."

I shot a glance at Jake, who was holding his little finger up in the air and with the other hand was pushing his nose up. Debra made a face and shook her head a little.

So Miss Jean's sister was a snob, but I knew we had to live with it, so I said, "Hey, I'm really glad you've come, Miss Ellen! We've got more to do than we can say grace over trying to get these two hitched. You can really be a help."

"Ellen's done lots of weddings, Barney," Miss Jean said with a smile. "And she's offered to do anything she can for ours."

"That's great!" I said, nodding. "I guess the

117

first thing is the wedding rehearsal tomorrow night."

"I assume that's to be in the church?" Miss Ellen asked.

"Well, actually it's not," I said. "The church is still being remodeled, so we'll have to have the actual rehearsal somewhere else."

"I see." Her lips got a little tight. "Exactly where will this rehearsal take place?"

"Well. . . ," I stammered a little and had to clear my throat. ". . . We had a little trouble finding a place. What we finally decided was to have it at Mr. Hitchcock's barn."

"You're going to have the wedding rehearsal in a barn!"

"I know it sounds pretty bad, but it's the best we can do. And it's a nice barn— concrete floor and everything."

"I'm sure it's *charming!*" Ellen said with a shrug. She gave Miss Jean a look as if to say, "Well, you've certainly found a nice bunch of bumpkins! What else can you expect!"

But Miss Jean was so happy she paid no attention to her sister. She was hanging onto Coach's arm, looking at him with a big smile. I don't think she'd have noticed if we'd had the wedding on top of the courthouse.

Which might have been a smart thing to do—considering the way things turned out!

I was so busy getting things lined up for the wedding that I didn't see Miss Jean's sister again until all of us met at Mr. Hitchcock's barn, but Debra and Tippi told me all about her. We were in my pickup riding to the barn at the time.

"She's the world's most awful snob!" Debra said, her eyes flashing. "I don't think she's Miss Jean's sister at all!"

"Probably the Fletchers found her under a toadstool," Tippi said. "She hasn't said *one* nice thing about the wedding or Coach Littlejohn or anything!"

I shrugged and said, "Well, I guess it does seem pretty primitive to a lady from Boston—a wedding rehearsal in a barn. Come on. I think we're late."

We got out of my pickup and crossed the snow, being careful not to slip on the glassy surface. No snow had fallen for a couple of days, but more was on the way.

"Too bad the honeymoon couldn't be in Biloxi like you planned," Debra said, grabbing my arm to keep from falling. "It's nice and warm there."

Tippi grabbed my other arm, also to keep from falling. "Where are they going?"

"Well, at first they were planning to go down to the railroad and chunk rocks," I said. Both girls were hanging onto me like leeches, and I was glad to get to the barn door and shake them off. "Then Jake had a great idea for once. He thought about a cabin that belongs to Debra's granddad. It's way up in the mountains toward Mount Ida, so he talked with Uncle Dave and that's where they're going."

"It's real neat!" Debra said. "Granddad never did much with it, but Daddy fixed it up real nice two years ago so we could all go there for vacations."

Debra's father had more money than he had hair, so if he fixed it up, it would be nice.

"That's one worry off my mind," I said, scraping the packed snow off my feet. "Now if we can just get through this wedding, I can die happy."

We went into the barn, and everybody else was there waiting. Brother Roberts, the pastor, waved his big hand at us and called out, "Get a move on, Barney, before we all freeze to death!"

Fortunately the barn was nice and clean because Mr. Hitchcock hadn't used it for a couple of years. But it was colder than a well diggers feet! The temperature was below freezing, and I could see my breath as we went over and joined the party.

Mrs. Roberts was there to help, and Miss Jean had three local girls as her bridesmaids, and Coach had picked three of his buddies to pair off with them as groomsmen. Coach and Miss Jean were so wrapped up in each other they forgot to be cold.

But Ellen Fletcher looked like the White Witch of the North! She was wrapped up in a fur coat, with just her nose and eyes peeking out of a hood, and I could tell she thought we were all nutty as a pecan orchard.

But it went all right. I mean it was cold and a little uncomfortable, but actually it was one of those crazy times when so many things go wrong that everybody gets flaky and sort of hysterical. Even the preacher got so tickled he couldn't get through his part.

Finally after about an hour he stopped laughing long enough to say, "Look. Let's go through this one more time, then go eat. I think the more we work on it, the worse it gets!"

"But, Reverend, what about all the mistakes?" Ellen asked. She was the only one who hadn't laughed, and she was so upset her cheeks were getting red. "I mean, it's a *disaster!*"

Brother Roberts took a long look at her, then smiled. "Miss Fletcher, I've been in a thousand weddings. Some of them went smoothly, but most of them broke down at some point or another. But one thing I can promise you. . . ." He turned to smile at Coach and Miss Jean. ". . . No matter *what* goes wrong—I don't care if the building falls down—when we leave the church you'll be man and wife!"

Well, we all got into our places, and it went off like clockwork! I mean no one messed up and it was looking good.

Until Ulysses got into the act.

Ulysses was Mr. Hitchcock's prize bull, a

fine steel grey Santa Gertrudis—that meant he was one-half Brahman. He wasn't any longer than a four-door sedan, but then he wasn't much smaller either!

He was tame as a kitten, though, and would wander around the Hitchcock farm like a pet coon. This time he must have heard the noise inside the barn and nosed the back door open, but nobody heard him come in. Big as they are, those bulls can be as quiet as a mouse.

I was standing way up at the front with Coach and Miss Ellen, who had just marched down the aisle in time with the music that we played on a cassette recorder. It was up pretty loud, and I guess that was why we hadn't heard Ulysses come in.

Ellen got to the front, turned to her left, and walked over to the far right. That put her close to the line of doors that made up the individual stalls that ranged along the sides of the barn, not over ten feet from one door that was open.

I don't know why I looked over there, but I did—and what I saw just about paralyzed me!

Ulysses had come drifting through the door and was standing right behind Miss Ellen!

He was nosey like always, and when he saw that big furry thing in front of him, I guess he just wanted to taste it. So he stretched his neck and opened his big old mouth and nibbled at the back of Miss Ellen's head. Not too hard, but tasting, you know?

Miss Ellen felt something touching the back of her head and turned around to see what it was. What she saw was this monster towering over her, with a set of horns that ended in needle points and a mouth that looked like the Holland Tunnel—and all this not six inches away from her face.

I don't think she believed what she was seeing at first—maybe thought she was having some kind of a colossal nightmare. She froze, and I started over there to get Ulysses out of the barn, when he reached out gave her a big moist lick on the face with his tongue, which was about the size of a blanket.

That broke the trance, all right! She let out a holler that put a Missouri Pacific engine to shame and took off running away from Ulysses! Everybody jumped and started looking around, but I was the only one who'd seen Ulysses come in. I made a run to catch up with Miss Ellen, but I was too late, because she ran right into the wall and bounced off to sit down flat on the floor, screaming her head off!

All the screaming scared Ulysses, who tried to get out of the barn, but got mixed up. He forgot where the door was and made a run right at the middle of the wedding party. The group scattered like drops of water when you stomp a puddle of water.

Almost everybody got out of the way, but Coach was trying to get Miss Jean clear when he got bumped by Ulysses. That little bump sent him flying right into one of the upright beams that held up the roof.

Brother Roberts was the one I couldn't take my eyes off of, though. I'd gone over to Miss Ellen, but when I glanced back, there was my pastor rising in the air!

He had been right in Ulysses' path, but instead of dodging right or left, he'd grabbed a rope that was dangling from a rafter and was now scrambling up that thing like a monkey with his tail swinging! I never knew they taught you how to climb a rope like that at the seminary!

But it was Tiny who saved the day! He noticed Ulysses was scared and liable to hurt someone, so he ran to the bull, took him by one of those horns, and started talking to him in a gentle voice. Ulysses was so spooked he tossed his head, but Tiny held on, and although Ulysses was flapping around like a silk necktie in the breeze, Tiny got him quiet.

Miss Ellen had stopped screaming, too, so that helped. I pulled her up on her feet and her mouth was opening and closing like a catfish out of water, but she wasn't hurt.

"Ellen!" Jean cried when she came over and put her arms around her sister. "Are you all right?"

Miss Ellen Fletcher of Boston must have had a little of her sister's character. She made herself stop sniveling and managed to get a proper look on her face. "Oh, certainly, Jean.

After all, what's a little thing like getting gored by a wild beast at a simple wedding rehearsal?"

Coach laughed and went over to give his almost sister-in-law a big hug. "Sure, Ellen, but you mustn't plan on having as much fun as this *every* time I get married!"

You know what? Bad as it was, that brush with Ulysses sort of broke the ice between Miss Ellen Fletcher and the rest of us. She was still pretty snooty, but if she got around a good man like Coach, he could sweet-talk her out of it.

"Well, Jake, let's eat," I said when we got all sorted out. "Where's the dinner?"

Jake had been "negotiating," as he called it, with several restaurants, but it had come right down to the wire.

"Well, it was pretty close." Jake nodded with that smug look he got whenever he thought he'd done something wonderful. "I got a good offer from the Gables—"

"Hey, they serve great food!" Joe said.

"But they were a little high. And the Bonanza had a pretty good deal, but I got a better one."

"For crying out loud, Jake, where are we going to eat?" I asked.

"At the Dew Drop Inn!" he announced proudly.

"The Dew Drop Inn!" I gasped. "Jake, that's a *truck stop!*"

"Yeah, but my theory is that you can either

have food or atmosphere for your money," Jake said. "You see, when you go to a real fancy restaurant, you have to pay for all the setting. But when you go to a *modest* place, why they soak the money into good food instead of atmosphere, you see?"

"Well, the Dew Drop Inn is 'modest' enough," Coach said with a grin. He was tickled over the choice, I could see, and he added, " 'Never eat at a place called Mom's and never play cards with a man named Doc'—that's my motto. But the Dew Drop Inn has one of the best burgers in the county."

"Sure and the waitress has a new hairdo, just for *us*," Jake said proudly, "and they have new linoleum, too."

"Let's go," I said. "I sure do hope the booth's not taken!"

We drove to the Dew Drop Inn, which was on Interstate 40, and the place was crowded with truck drivers as always. But May Jones who ran the place had put four of the square tables together at the back and covered them with red-and-white checkered tablecloths. We took our seats and began studying the menu, then settled down for a good evening.

Of course the jukebox was a little loud, and some of the songs weren't quite what you'd expect at this kind of dinner. One of them was a tune called "I Lost Freida on the Freeway." It was about this couple who just got married in Los Angeles, and they'd gone to the church in two cars. Then the bride got in her car and the groom in his, intending to leave one of them and take off for Niagara Falls. But Freida made a wrong turn and got off the freeway. The groom got off at the next exit, and when he was roaring back, he saw Freida going in the opposite direction looking for *him!* So they just went on and on like that, and they never got together, just always looking for each other.

"Gosh, it gets you right *here!*" Coach sighed, putting his hand over his heart and trying to look sad.

"That's not where it gets *me,*" I said, but Debra shook her head at me so I hushed.

We had a great meal and got to hear the truck drivers talk, which is always *colorful*, and after we ate we made our final plans.

"Jake, I'm worried about the clothes," I said. "Here it is the night before our wedding, and we don't have a thing to wear."

"Don't worry, Barney." Jake waved his hand in the air. "I got a great deal. Got all the right sizes, and they'll be here at eight in the morning. Got 'em from the Dillman Company. You know how good *they* are!"

"Well, they're the best," I said.

"And you don't have to worry about the special effects, either," Joe said. "Mr. McCoy and I have had a few problems, but when the wedding starts, everything will be working fine."

"What's *everything*, Joe?" I asked.

"Oh, you know, special music, lighting, and

127

stuff like that. You don't even have to think about it. I'll be at the control board and take care of everything."

Joe was as reliable as the earth, so I said, "All right, then, all systems are *go!* Synchronize your watches, men, and it's over the top at eight o'clock sharp tomorrow!"

We all got up to leave, but Ellen pulled me off to one side, and for once there was a little smile on her face. She was a good-looking woman when she wasn't all puckered up.

"Barney, I want to apologize for being such a stinker when I first got here. I guess I was just about sick with worry over the marriage—not knowing Dale very well. But I can see he's just what Jean needs."

"Sure, he's the best!"

"And the wedding, well, Jean told me how you boys are doing this all on your own, and I want to thank you for it. I know it's been hard, and you've done a great job with nothing to work with—money, I mean."

"Sure, well—"

"There's just *one* thing I think you ought to change."

"What's that?"

"Well, I know that Tiny is a nice young man. . . ." She bit her lip, then went on, "I–I don't want to sound awful, but do you think it's wise to let him be in the wedding? I mean, won't he be likely to do something wrong?"

"Look, Miss Ellen, most people leave disaster to chance," I said. "We're not going to make that mistake. *Something* is almost sure to go wrong at any wedding, so we're going to have what I call a *controlled* disaster. I mean by that, we know that Tiny's likely to do something wrong, but we can watch him. That way we know where the trouble's going to be. That's *my* idea. What do you think?"

She gave me a really nice smile, then threw her arms around me and gave me a hug!

"I think you're a fine young man!" she said. "And no matter what happens at the wedding, Jean is lucky to have you!"

What is this strange power I have over women?

TEN
In Living Color

"Barney! Where are the tuxes and the dresses?"

Miss Ellen caught up with me as I was trying to carry one of the big flower stands to the front of the church. She was wringing her hands, and from the look on her face she hadn't slept much.

"Jake said they'd be here by noon, Miss Ellen."

"But we won't be able to do much more than try them on, Barney! What if they don't fit?"

"No sweat." I put the heavy flower stand down and tried to look a lot more confident than I felt. I hadn't slept much myself, and now that the zero hour was approaching, I was pretty shaky. "We all got measured a month ago. It'll be all right."

"But how will—"

"Trust me! It's going to be a wedding long to be remembered, Miss Ellen."

I patted her shoulder and muscled the flower stand up to the front of the auditorium. I had to squeeze past Mr. McCoy, who was installing some sort of device in the middle of the floor. He looked up at me with his toothless grin and nodded happily. "Goin' good, ain't it, boy?"

I didn't have time to answer, because just as I opened my mouth, a blunt object hit me right on the head!

"Look out, Barney!" Too late.

I rubbed my aching head and stared up to see Joe hanging onto a set of ropes like a monkey. He was doing something to a big chandelier, and he hollered, "Toss me up that wrench, will ya, Barney?"

"So you can brain me again?" I tossed it up and asked, "Are you about through with all the wiring and stuff, Joe?"

"Well, we've had a few problems, but we'll have them all worked out soon."

I shook my head and put the flowers in place. Taking a look around, I saw that things were going pretty well. The big candelabras were set up, flowers were in place, the ribbons on the front pews were all taped on—everything looked good.

"Hey, the truck from Dillman's is here!"

I ran back to the Fellowship Hall, where Jake was helping a guy pile a bunch of boxes and stuff on a table.

"I told you they'd be here on time!" Jake gloated. He signed the ticket for the delivery man, and then we all crowded around to see the dresses and the tuxes. "I don't want to brag, folks, but I gotta say that for us to get our duds from a fancy place like Dillman's—and for *free*—well, you can save the applause!"

"I can't figure out how you got all these clothes for nothing," Coach said. "Never knew that place to give anything away." We all crowded around him as he found the box with his name on it and ripped it open. When the top came off and he pulled the tissue paper out, he stood there staring at it, not saying a word.

There was a funny look on his face, so I asked, "What's the matter, Coach?"

He looked up and said, "Well, I've been to three county fairs, two snake-stompings, and a bunch of weddings, but I've never seen anything to equal *this!*"

He pulled his coat out of the box, and a gasp went around the room. Then there was silence. Finally, Tiny said, "That sure is a pretty pink coat, Coach!"

Pink! It was a beautiful shade of rosy pink!

"Coach, that can't be *your* tux!" I sputtered.

"My name's on the box," he said.

"Hey, look at this!" Tiny said in delight. "Mine is my favorite color—green!" He was holding his tux up, and sure enough, it was the brightest green I'd ever seen!

There was a furor as we all dug into the boxes. In a few seconds the room looked like a rainbow gone wild—red, orange, green, purple—you name it!

I held up the bright blue tux that had my name on it and felt sick. "Jake, I know it may sound unreasonable to you, but do you think you could explain a little bit about why you picked out all these weird colors?"

Jake grinned and said, "It's great! What happened was that this rich Chinese family had this real fancy wedding in Little Rock. And they like bright colors at their weddings. So Dillman had them left over and they offered to alter them and let me have them for free—well, almost free."

"Almost?"

"Well, I had to agree that they could come and take pictures during the wedding. I think they're going to do a big splash in the *Arkansas Gazette* pretty soon."

I felt like the floor was opening up. "You mean to stand there with your face hanging out and tell me we're going to have our pictures in the state paper dressed up in *these!*"

"No extra charge, Barney," Jake said with a grin. "It's *great*, isn't it?"

"It's a *disaster!*" Ellen wailed. She held up a bright red dress and moaned, "I can't wear this thing!"

Well, things got pretty thick, and I thought we'd have to get a doctor for Miss Ellen, but finally Coach took over.

"Look, this is no big deal," he said. "Jean will be wearing her mother's wedding dress, and that's the important thing. I don't care if I have to wear a pair of overalls."

"I'd *rather* wear overalls than this thing!" I complained. "We'll look like circus clowns!"

"Barney, it's all right," Coach said with a smile. "If I can wear a pink tux, the rest of you can wear what you've got." His eyes lit up and he laughed out loud. "Who knows, maybe we'll start a new trend!"

Debra held up a dress about the same shade as a bad bruise. "I hope a chameleon doesn't get loose during the wedding," she said with a grin. "He'd go crazy trying to match up with us!"

The rest of the day was a blur to me. I seem to remember a lot of people running around shaking their heads and saying, "It can't be done!"

Somehow, though, I found myself standing in a room with Coach and his best man at eight o'clock. He had a pretty tense look on his face and seemed to have some trouble breathing.

"Well, I've got to go, Coach," I said. "Now don't worry. It's going to be great!"

I left and hurried down the hall in time to be grabbed by Miss Ellen. "Barney, where have you been? Never mind. There's your cue to go light the candles. Hurry up! Tiny's got your lighter!"

I hurried down the hall to meet Tiny, who handed me the brass butane lighter. He asked me with a big grin, "All set, Barney?"

"I guess so."

You know how it goes. We went down to the front by separate aisles carrying the silver candles. The church was packed, and when I heard a murmur in the crowd, I knew it was the sight of the green and blue tuxes that Tiny and I were wearing.

We made our way to the front of the church, and then Tiny took his place in front of his candles and I did the same with mine. I was a little shaky lighting my first candle, but as I did the others, I got a little more steady.

By the time I'd gotten about half of my candles lit, I began to feel that something was wrong. From my left there was a *clicking* sound. I glanced around and saw that Tiny was trying to relight his lighter.

I slowed down so we'd finish together, but the clicking sound broke through the silence. I think everybody in the church was holding his breath, hoping that Tiny would get that thing going.

Finally, he turned to me and asked in a hoarse whisper that could be heard all over the church, "Hey, Barney, you got a match?"

"No!"

We'd given Tiny the easiest job, but now I didn't know what to do!

"OK, I found one."

I glanced out of the corner of my eye and saw that he'd fished a kitchen match out of his pocket. The church had spent a lot of money having the auditorium redecorated, and when Tiny raked the match right across the top rail and gouged a scratch, I heard the entire board of deacons take a deep breath.

The match spurted a blue flame, and Tiny got his lighter going. He was back in business. He started lighting the candles, but in the process he also threw the match on the new carpet right under a set of new drapes.

I didn't notice it at first because I was finishing my own candles. But there was a stir in the crowd—sort of a running whisper. Then just as I lit my last candle, somebody cried out, "Fire!"

I looked around and saw a little tongue of flame leaping at the lower edge of the drape, and then I just stood there paralyzed!

But Tiny didn't. He heard the cry, and when he looked down and saw the curtain and the rug on fire, he went into action. Dropping the butane lighter, he started beating at the flame with his hands. Since it was only a small flame, he managed to get it out at once.

But the butane lighter had touched off another section of the drapes by this time. I started to help, but Tiny took one look and without wasting a single motion ripped a tablecloth off the table on the platform and proceeded to beat the fire out, at the same time choking and practically strangling himself in the smoke!

Unfortunately the tablecloth had been under a silver tray holding a service that had been intended for communion. The cups went sailing out into the first row of pews, hitting Mrs. Ellie Dinwiddie in the ear, and she set up a wild howl!

It wasn't exactly the most graceful beginning for a wedding, but somehow I managed to get Tiny pulled together and we beat a retreat down the aisles.

In the vestibule, Miss Ellen had a glazed look in her eyes, but she forced a grin and said with a shrug, "Well, at least we didn't have to call the fire department."

"No, but it's not over yet," I said weakly.

"There's the cue for the bridesmaids and groomsmen!" she whispered. She pushed me into the line and said, "Try not to do anything else wrong."

We waited while Coach and his best man, along with Pastor Roberts, came out of a back room and took their places on the platform. Then Miss Ellen said, "All right, go!"

What we were supposed to do was a little different from most weddings. Coach and Miss Jean wanted to get as many friends as they could involved, so Miss Ellen came up with the idea of having couples walk down the aisle arm in arm—both aisles at the same time. Then we'd all meet at the front.

It had been an impressive idea, and with all the wild colors we had, it made a pretty picture.

Of course I couldn't see much of it. Jake and Judy Grimes had started out on the aisle I was on. Right behind them were Tiny and Tippi. I could see that Tippi had a death grip on Tiny's arm to keep him from messing up.

Well, we did fine! Somewhere up in the balcony Joe was sitting in a control booth. He faded the lights in and out so that it was really pretty—especially me in my blue tux! And he did a good job with the music, too. He'd rigged up speakers all over the place, and instead of an organ there was a great orchestra that came out of the stereo, flooding the church with music.

I actually got to enjoying it! We were in perfect time. Miss Ellen had drilled us hard on that. I didn't have a lot of rhythm myself, but Debra did, and she kept me right on the beat.

To explain what happened next, you have to understand that a new air-conditioning system had just been installed in the church. The air came in through ducts in the floor, and these were covered by grates with very fine grids. Several of these had been installed in the aisles, and they had been no trouble at all.

Not until Judy Grimes stepped into one of them with her high heel.

I couldn't see what was happening, of course. No one could, but I heard about it later.

There was Judy hanging on to Jake with her new high heels on. She was keeping perfect time when suddenly her heel went down in the grid and she found her foot caught as if it was in a steel trap!

She said later, "I didn't know what to do! I mean, I could have bent over and tried to pull it out, but it was stuck too tight for that. So in a flash, I made a decision. I just slipped my foot out of my shoe and without missing a beat went on down the aisle!"

That was pretty slick, or it would have been if Tiny hadn't been right behind Judy.

He saw what was happening, and he made a decision, too. Without missing a beat or a step, he got to Judy's shoe, and still in perfect time, he bent over and picked it right up!

The only thing was that the shoe was stuck tight, and the grid hadn't been fastened down. So Tiny picked up both the shoe *and* the grid.

Then here I came with Debra, giving all my attention to keeping in perfect time. And in perfect time, I stepped right into the open hole!

Debra said she didn't know what happened. Part of me just disappeared, and there I was sitting on the floor with one leg out in front of me and the other one up to my hip in a hole in the floor.

The couple behind us, in perfect time, had the sense to split. One went to my left and one to my right.

I jerked and yanked, but somehow I was stuck so tight I couldn't get loose.

"Barney, will you stop that fooling!" Debra whispered.

Tiny must have heard her. I saw him whip his head around, and as soon as he saw the mess I was in, he came stampeding back dragging Tippi like the tail on a kite.

"Barney! You done went and lost your leg!" he said sympathetically.

"No, I'm just stuck!"

He stared at me, then laughed so loud the chandelier trembled. "Shoot! I thought you'd lost it!"

He took me under the arms and gave such a pull that I almost *did* lose a leg, but he popped me loose.

"There!" he said with a grin. He scurried back to his place, and seeing that everybody was staring, he waved a hand and yelled, "It's OK! Barney just got stuck in a hole!"

Well, that did distract from the pageantry of the thing, but with a burning face, I let Debra pull me along. Somehow we finally all made it to the front and took our places.

I'd sat in the choir a few times at church, and it always amazed me to see how bored some people looked in the congregation. But as the flashbulbs kept popping off, I noticed there wasn't a bored face at *this* wedding!

As Uncle Dave Simmons put it later: "It was a real good show! Sort of a political convention, a circus, a bad traffic accident, a rip-snorting revival, and a county fair all rolled up in one!"

ELEVEN
Here Comes the Bride!

Maybe everything will go right from here on, I thought as I stood at the front of the church, waiting for Miss Jean to come down the aisle. *After all, you can only cram so much disaster into one little bitty wedding, and maybe we've already had our share.*

I glanced down the line at Tiny to make sure he didn't pull anything. He was OK. Nothing to worry about there.

A movement up high in the balcony caught my eye. There were Joe and Mr. McCoy sitting in the control booth. Joe saw me looking at him and gave me a V for victory sign.

I drew a deep sigh of relief, and then the music we'd been waiting for came over the speakers—"Here Comes the Bride!"

The doors opened, and Miss Jean stepped

into the sanctuary, leaning on the arm of her uncle, Mr. Don Fletcher.

Everybody in the church stood up and turned to watch her as she came toward the front, and she was something! Her mother's dress was white, of course, and she looked like a delicate cloud as she marched down the aisle. I caught a glimpse of Coach's face. You'd have thought he'd gone to heaven!

I couldn't help thinking how nice it was going to be to have a set of parents like these two! As she got closer, I forgot to be worried. I just stood there grinning like mad.

Then, just as Miss Jean got almost to where Coach was standing, the music sort of faded out, and there was a squeal that nearly burst my ears. Then a rough voice blared out, "Hey, good buddy! I think I done spotted me a couple of smokies!"

Then there was another squeaking roar, and another voice thundered: "Roger! I got me some bear bait, but keep me up to snuff, good buddy! Ten four!"

Miss Jean's face turned pale and her jaw dropped, but she swallowed and stepped up to stand with Coach.

Glancing up at the control booth, I saw Joe twisting knobs like crazy! I knew immediately that he'd gotten some wires crossed in the speaker system and was picking up truck drivers using their CBs.

Brother Roberts looked like he'd bitten into an underripened persimmon, but he'd been a chaplain in the Marines during the Viet Nam War, so I guess he figured he could handle it. He opened his mouth, but instead of his voice, we heard another roar of static. Then came the words:

"Hey, Al, catch this squeal, will ya?"

"What's going down, Fred?"

I recognized the voices of Albert Tennie and Fred Sloan, two of our local policemen, and I hoped fervently they'd shut up!

"They's a couple of suspicious-looking characters hanging around at the church. Check them out, hey?"

I thought Coach and Miss Jean would fall through the floor when they heard that, and a simper went up from a few knotheads who would have laughed when the *Titanic* had sunk!

Joe pulled a bunch of wires loose and stood there looking like a snake handler holding a bunch of snakes as he glared at the control board. He must have gotten the right ones, because there was no more police talk or truck drivers, either.

Brother Roberts started talking real fast, probably trying to head off any more messages from anybody. "Beloved, we are gathered here this evening to celebrate the union of Dale Littlejohn and Jean Fletcher."

He slowed down after awhile, when he realized that Joe had gotten the speakers under control. For a long time he talked about how marriage is a holy matter and should not be entered into lightly.

I was listening to him, but at the same time, I was admiring the way Joe was handling the lights. I knew he'd spent a lot of time putting in dimmer switches so that he could bring the lights up or slowly make them fade. And it looked good, too!

He'd also put in some colored lights. As the service went on, he faded the side lights almost off, and there was a glow that came down from the huge chandelier that was directly over the pulpit. It was a mass of tiny glass bulbs. It was really beautiful the way Joe faded them down until there was just a trace of a rosy glow bathing the group below! Then I noticed that people were staring up at the chandelier.

I was trying to keep my mind on what Brother Roberts was saying, but you know how it is when a thing like that happens. (Once a cat got on the stage when we were having our high school graduation, and nobody heard a word anybody said! They all watched that fool cat as he chased his tail and took a bath right at the side of the speaker's platform!)

More and more people were craning their necks to stare at the chandelier over our heads, and I rolled my eyes up to see what was attracting all the attention.

The chandelier was revolving!

It wasn't going very fast, just slowly turning like a huge wheel. I knew right away that it was something that Joe had worked up to give the wedding a little class, and I glanced at the control booth in a panic.

Mr. McCoy and Joe were staring at the chandelier and nodding. Both of them were smiling with satisfaction, and I wagged my head trying to get Joe's attention. I wanted to signal him to shut the thing off, but he was happy with it!

Brother Roberts knew something was going on. I never knew how he did it, but he could preach to a congregation of 500 people and know just which boy in the whole crowd was doing something he shouldn't.

I guess Miss Jean and Coach were too caught up in what Brother Roberts was saying to pay attention, and anyway, they had their backs to the crowd.

I raised my hand as if to scratch my ear and waved a little at Joe. He caught it, then grinned and waved right back.

I framed the words silently with my lips: *Shut it off!*

He nodded and grinned like an idiot, thinking I was bragging on his great idea!

About that time I heard a whirring sound. Looking up again, I noticed that the chandelier had picked up speed! It was going fast enough now to create a noise, and Joe had noticed it, too. I sighed with relief when he reached out and threw a switch.

Instead of stopping, though, the spinning chandelier picked up speed!

By then every eye in the church was on that thing, including those of the bride and groom. Brother Roberts knew his ceremony by heart so he kept right on with it, but all of us stood there as the chandelier came on full power and the whirring sound changed to a high-pitched scream!

Without warning, one of the light bulbs flew out of its socket, then shot across the auditorium and shattered against the wall with a loud crash. There was another and then another until before long it sounded like the first day of hunting season!

Brother Roberts suddenly slammed his Bible shut and in a voice that almost shook the plaster off the wall shouted, "Joe! Stop that fool thing!"

I saw Joe swallow. Then he yanked another handful of wires out of the board. The chandelier went dark suddenly, then coasted to a stop.

"Now, maybe we can get on with this wedding!" Brother Roberts said loudly. He opened his book and began speaking in a milder tone.

"Every couple should have a love song, and Jean and Dale have theirs. We're going to pause now and listen to the song that these two want to be a symbol of their love for each other."

I knew that both of them loved an old song

called "Together." It's a neat song about two people staying in love as long as they are on this earth.

Joe reached out and punched a button, but "Together" was *not* the song that came over the speakers!

I guess he must have gotten one of Mr. McCoy's tapes by mistake, because what blared out was a brassy-voiced country singer who sang a little ditty called, "You Done Tore My Heart Out and Stomped That Sucker Flat!"

Well, Joe moved like lightening! He yanked out another bunch of wires, and then there was this awful silence. It was real tense, with nobody knowing what to do.

Then right out of that silence came a clear voice, pure as silver, singing the words that Miss Jean and Coach loved so well, "We always will be together."

I nearly fell off the platform, because it was Debra standing right beside me who was singing!

I knew she could sing well, but for her to pull that song out at that moment was really something! We all listened to her as the song talked about how two people needed each other when they were young and when they were old. In troubled or good times, and then it ended by giving God the glory for their lives together.

There wasn't a dry eye in the house when she got to the last line "We always will be together."

A spontaneous amen went up from all over the house, and I just had to reach out and give her a squeeze even though I knew I'd get kidded about it later!

The next thing was the exchange of vows by the bride and groom, and I thought to myself, *At least nothing can mess this up!*

Wrong!

Part of the remodeling of the church included redoing the rostrum—that was where the pulpit and choir loft were located—into something that could be used for church drama. The whole thing was built so that scenery could be moved into place as we'd done for the Christmas play.

The part that I didn't know about was "the lift," but I found out about it pretty fast!

Lots of drama events needed a part of the stage—like a cellar door or something like that—to open up. Mr. McCoy and Joe had worked it out so that the spot where Brother Roberts was standing fit the bill.

A switch in the control room activated a motor, and the section where he was standing would begin sinking right into the basement. Reverse the switch, and the section would *rise* about ten feet in the air.

Every eye was on the bride and groom when all of a sudden my heart gave a lurch as I saw Brother Roberts sinking into the floor!

I blinked my eyes and shook my head, but he just kept on going down—down—down!

A murmur of amazement rose from the congregation, and I guess the whole thing must have come as quite a shock to Brother Roberts, who knew nothing about the lift. His years in the Marines must have prepared him for anything, though, because he just kept on talking. Talking and sinking slowly into the dark depths of the basement!

". . . So you two must be true to one another. Therefore, I require you Dale and you Jean to make your vows public at this time. . . ." By the time he got to the end of his statement, Brother Roberts was nothing but a memory. All that was left of him was a hollow voice coming from somewhere in the depths of the building!

I glanced up at the control board where Joe and Mr. McCoy were working like mad to get the pastor out of the hole!

We kept hearing his voice rumbling in a ghostly, hollow tone from somewhere in the depths, and then I guess Joe found the switch that would bring him back to us, but he pushed it too hard or something.

Brother Roberts shot up out of the basement like a missile lifting off at Cape Canaveral! He got to the level of the first floor, but then Joe must have missed his cue, because we all popped our necks watching as Brother Roberts rode the platform up and up until he was perched there about ten feet over the heads of the bride and groom.

It was a tense moment, as you can well imagine.

Eventually, Brother Roberts shut his book with a loud thump and leaned over to peer down at Coach and Miss Jean. Then he looked up at the control booth.

"Joseph Buck, do you think you might do *something* to bring me back to the land of the living? I'd like to join the rest of you and get this couple married!"

Joe fumbled around, then finally pushed the right switch and down came Brother Roberts, eager to settle back on the same plane as all the rest of us.

He looked around with a smile, then fixed his eyes on Dale and Miss Jean. "I suppose you young people are very upset over all these . . . inconveniences. And no one could blame you. I must say you have stood the fiery trial." Then his voice got very serious.

"Dale and Jean, you are beginning a new life, and you have both been exposed to a lot of romantic stories about marriage. I want to tell you that when you said, 'For better or for worse,' in the sight of God you committed yourself to exactly *that!* But I want you to know that your lives may very well be much like this wedding!"

I heard a voice that sounded a lot like Miss Ellen's say faintly, "Oh, no!"

"Most of us here are well aware that you two intend to make a home for three boys. I

must say that I admire your faith. . . ."
Brother Roberts glanced around, and I felt
that he was turning a spotlight on me!
". . . For rearing these particular boys will be
a task that would test the patience of Job!"

"Amen!" about ten people in the
congregation said fervently.

Then the pastor held up his hand and said,
"God is going to bless your marriage, because
you have given him your lives. Now, you are
ready to begin. Repeat after me, 'I Dale, take
thee, Jean, for my wedded wife. . . .' "

After they said their vows, the pastor said,
"By the authority vested in me by the State
of Arkansas, I pronounce you husband and
wife! You may kiss the bride."

Coach kissed her, and there was a big burst
of applause from all of us, something I'd
never seen at a wedding before!

I leaned over and said to Debra, "Well,
that's over. Nothing can go wrong *now!*"

Wrong again!

Jake had one more idea that had sounded
good at the time (typical of his nutty
schemes). He had the idea of releasing a dove
just as the couple left the altar and were
proceeding down the aisle. He said it would
symbolize a new life set free or something.

Anyway, the bridesmaids helped Miss Jean
get her train all fixed and then Joe played
the final music and they started down the
aisle. Jake reached over and picked up the
birdcage and opened the door.

It was sort of nice to see that white dove (which was really a pigeon since we couldn't get a dove) flutter out and land on the back of a pew.

Actually, it would have been better if the bird had flown up to the balcony.

What happened was that Mr. McCoy had a mangy old tom cat named Dillinger, who mooched around the church most of the time. Anyway, he'd been taking a nap behind the organ. When the blast of music started, he woke up, and when he stuck his head around the corner, there was this nice juicy pigeon just begging to be munched!

Dillinger made two jumps.

First, he made it from the organ to within striking distance of the bird by landing on the back of Coach's best man—Ralph Wilson. He dug his claws into Ralph's shoulder and neck, and Ralph let out a yell like a wounded Indian!

Then Dillinger made the second leg of his hunt by landing in the lap of Matilda Lapwing, a deaf old lady who always sat in the front row and snored. As a matter of fact, she was sound asleep when Dillinger knocked the pigeon into her face with one swipe, and she woke up with her mouth full of feathers and her lap full of cat trying to slaughter an innocent bird.

It was probably the most excited Miss Lapwing ever got in church, and she let out a screech like a fire engine!

Dillinger got confused and so did the bird, so they both wandered back and forth around the room, giving everybody sort of a scare.

Finally, the bird got sense enough to fly up to the balcony and that was that.

Brother Roberts was standing there just shaking his head. When the excitement was over, he said, "You are all invited to attend a reception in honor of the bride and groom in the Fellowship Hall." He looked around at me, then at Jake, and finally up at Joe.

"The Buck brothers are in charge of it. The trouble will start in fifteen minutes!" He shook his head slowly and added, "Attend at your own risk."

TWELVE
Taking
the Cake

The Fellowship Hall was packed, of course,
and by the time I'd stood in the reception line
long enough to shake hands a million times, I
was ready to quit.

"Will you stop fidgeting!" Debra whispered
fiercely.

"I can't help it, Debra. This tie is choking
me to death! How long do we have to stand
here anyway?"

"Until everybody has had a chance to come
by and give you good wishes. Now behave!"

Well, actually it wasn't too bad, you know?
I mean three years ago we three hadn't had a
friend to speak of. Now people kept coming
by telling us nice things, and I could tell they
all meant it. I guess when my folks died all
three of us sorta gave up, but we hadn't been
at Goober Hollow too long before Uncle Dave

got me off to one side and told me that God was going to take care of us by giving us a family. It seemed too good to be true, but now it was here!

"Enough of this! Let's cut that cake!" Coach suddenly called out. He pulled his new bride to the big table where Tippi was standing beside a huge white cake flanked by two big punch bowls full of red punch.

"I hear you made this all by yourself, Tippi," Coach said, smiling at her.

She blushed and nodded, and I saw her father standing over by the wall looking real proud of her.

"I certainly hope you both like it," she said. "I did want to do something to help with the wedding."

"I'll bet it's the best refreshments any bride ever had," Miss Jean said and gave her a hug. "Hand me that knife and let's get started."

Tippi handed Miss Jean a silver knife with a broad blade, and we all watched as she sliced off a huge hunk and put it on a crystal plate. She handed it to Coach with a smile. "You're first, Dale."

"May it always be that way!" Coach laughed. He took up a huge chunk on a fork, opened his mouth until it looked like Mammoth Cave, and tossed the cake inside.

He took one bite, and then his eyes flew open. All of a sudden he spit out the whole thing and began hopping up and down, waving his arms around!

"Dale!" Miss Jean screamed. "What is it? What's wrong?"

He couldn't answer because he was spinning around like a top, and I saw that his face was as red as a fire engine!

"I think he's choked on the cake!"

"Couldn't be that!" I shouted. "He spit it all out!"

I tried to pat him on the back, but he pushed me aside, and then I saw his eyes light on the punch. With a roar he jumped to the table and stuck his head right into the punch bowl!

"He's gone crazy!" someone shouted, and it sure did look like it!

Finally, he pulled his head out of the punch bowl. His face was still red as fire, and with that red punch dripping down on his pink tux and his eyes all inflamed, he looked *wild!*

"What–what did–what did you put in the *cake!*" he finally managed to ask.

Tippi looked like a sheep-killing dog. "I–nothing, honest! I just put stuff that I found in your kitchen. It's a cinnamon cake, and I used flour, sugar, cinnamon, butter—"

"Wait a minute," I said. "Did you use the stuff in the jar marked *Cinnamon?*"

"Why, certainly I did."

"Yeah, well, I never use cinnamon for cooking, so that wasn't what was in that jar."

"What was in it, Barney?" Miss Jean asked.

"Well, that's where I keep all my ground-up hot peppers I use for my Mexican dishes."

Coach was looking a little green around the gills. He licked his lips and swallowed, then made a face. "Tippi, what was in the punch?"

"Just ginger ale, pop, and stuff like that."

"Wait a minute," I asked quickly. "You didn't get those ginger ale bottles on the back porch at our house did you?"

"You said I could use anything I found there, Barney!" Tippi said. She was getting some big tears in her eyes.

Coach stared at me and said feebly, "I'm afraid to ask."

"I am, too, Dale, but we have to know!" Miss Jean said. "What did you keep in those bottles, Barney?"

I cleared my throat and looked for a way to escape, but there wasn't any. "Oh, just the kerosene we used to start the fire with."

Coach turned almost as green as Tiny's tux. He nodded and said in a very small voice, "May I be excused for just a moment?" Without waiting any longer, he turned and walked across the room and out the door. He wasn't walking too steady, either!

We all just stood there, and it got real quiet. Everybody was trying not to stare at Miss Jean, who was standing there with the serving knife in her hand looking stunned.

Then all at once Tippi let out a wail like a fire alarm! "It's all my fault! I wish I was dead!"

I guess it was a pretty good thing she had a fit, because it gave Miss Jean something to do besides standing there holding the knife. She dropped it and ran over to put her arms around Tippi. "Now, you just stop that this minute, honey," she said. "It wasn't your fault at all." She gave me a look and added, "How in the world could you know anybody would put peppers in a cinnamon jar and kerosene in ginger ale bottles?"

"It's a real good thing she didn't get the stuff in the Coke bottles!" Jake piped up. "That *would* have been a mess!"

"What's in them?" Uncle Dave asked with a grin.

"Don't answer that! I don't want to know!" Miss Jean groaned. Then she smiled and said, "I can see that I'll have to be careful about what I put in my pies."

She was just great! Most women would have been swooning or screaming, but she just stood there, holding Tippi and acting like nothing was wrong.

We milled around for awhile, waiting for Coach to come back, and in about ten minutes Tiny came in with two big sacks.

"Look! I went and got refreshments!" he said with that big grin of his.

We all came to the table and he opened the sacks, saying, "I got lots of good stuff down at the store. Look, here's Ding Dongs . . . and Moon Pies and Snickers Bars . . . and potato chips and pretzels! And I got some root beer, and here's some Mr. Pibbs!"

"How wonderful!" Miss Jean said, and just

as Coach came back with his face almost a natural color, she threw her arms around Tiny and gave him a big smack! "What bride could ask for more than Moon Pies and Mr. Pibbs!"

Then it was Tiny's turn to blush, and we all pitched in and had a ball downing all the stuff Tiny had brought.

Finally, Coach said, "Well, I want to thank you all for coming—my wife and I both thank you!"

There was a cheer at that, and Miss Jean said, "There'll never be another wedding like this one!"

"Amen!" Brother Roberts said fervently. "This marriage has got to last—I've got too much *invested* in the wedding!"

Everybody laughed, and then Coach held up his hand. "Seriously, I want to tell you this. I think that I have a special blessing from God. A beautiful wife and three fine boys! And I didn't have to walk the floor or change a diaper to get them!"

Everybody laughed again, and then he said, "Several of you have told the Bucks how fortunate they are to have Jean and me as parents. . . ." Then he stopped and reached over and pulled me with one hand and Jake with the other and Miss Jean grabbed Joe and we all stood there in a tight little group. ". . . I want to tell you that Jean and I feel that *we* are the ones who are getting the blessing!"

Well, I hate to tell you this, but Joe started crying, and even Jake was swallowing and getting all choked up.

It didn't bother me, but I got something in my eye about that time and had to borrow a handkerchief from Coach to get rid of it.

Everybody was applauding and hugging us like crazy. All in all, it was about the finest thing that ever happened to old Barney Buck and his brothers!

"Boy, this is some place for a honeymoon!"

Jake, Joe, and I were standing in the middle of the large living room with its huge beams and the massive fireplace. None of us had seen the "cabin" that Mr. Simmons had fixed up, and we were stunned with the luxury of it.

"Hey, look at this—a sunken tub!" Joe had found one of the bathrooms, and we all went to look at the tub that looked like it would float a destroyer.

"Can you swim?" I said with a grin at our new mom.

"No. I better carry a life preserver before I get into that thing."

"Fear not," Coach grinned. "Wasn't I a hotshot lifeguard for three summers?"

They showed us through the house and it was a dream. We'd come over to the foothills of the Ozarks that shoot up next to Hot Springs, and we had to drive down five miles of county roads that hadn't been graded since

Washington was president, then up a hairpin mountain road for another two miles that zigzagged like nothing I ever saw to find the house!

We'd followed the newlyweds from the church in my pickup, but we had to get in the four-wheel drive Bronco to make the last couple of miles up the steep road. It was only about seven or eight feet wide, and I don't know what you'd do if you met another car. But then nobody used the place except the Simmonses or a friend from time to time.

"Hey, how about if I fix you a bridal supper before we split?" I asked. "I hate to come right out and *admit* it, but I'm just about the best in town at cooking steaks!"

"Well, I don't know," Coach said. "Looked like we might get some snow before morning. That road will be pretty slick."

"Aw, it won't take half an hour to fry up these goodies I picked out."

We all went into the kitchen and it was fun, but it took nearly two hours before we got the meal fixed and eaten and then all the mess cleaned up.

After that we sat down in front of the fire and just sort of digested and talked.

Finally, I got up and said, "Well, I hate to leave good company, but we'd better get home." I grinned at my new parents and added, "Unless you'd rather we stayed?"

"I'll get your coats," Coach said hurriedly.

We all put our coats on. Then just before

we went out the door, Miss Jean hugged the three of us and said, "Boys, I–I want you to be patient with me."

"Patient?" I asked.

"Well, I've been a social worker for a long time, and I've worked with lots of young people. But—well, that's different from having sons."

"Aw, you can handle the job," Jake said with a grin. "I knew you was a winner first time I laid eyes on you!"

"Sure, *Mom!*" Joe said and hugged her real hard. "It's going to be great having real parents!"

"*After* the honeymoon!" Coach said with a grin. "Now you all pile in, and I'll get you off this mountain."

We opened the door and stopped dead still. "Why, look at that!"

The moon had come out, and we saw that the ground was white with snow. The air was filled with huge flakes, and I stepped out to see how deep it was.

"Gosh, this stuff is two or three inches deep!"

"Dale, can you get down that road in snow like this?" Miss Jean asked.

He looked a little worried, then said, "If we didn't have four-wheel drive I wouldn't even try it, but I think it'll be all right if we take it easy."

We got in and she said in a worried voice, "I don't think you ought to try it, Dale."

"If it looks bad, I'll give it up as a bad job."

He put the Bronco in gear, but he'd only driven it but a couple of times and instead of forward, he accidentally put it in reverse. So, when he stepped on the gas to get us off the snow, we went *backward!*

I got a sinking feeling and Jean screamed, because we ran close to the sheer dropoff that was on the north end of the house. Mr. Simmons had stuck the house there just for the view, but it was a *long* way to the bottom!

I grabbed at Joe to try to break some of the fall. Then there was a loud *clunk* and we stopped. The front end of the car was hiked up, and when I peered out, I saw that the right edge of the bumper was wedged against a scrub oak tree about four inches thick. That was all that was holding us there!

"Be very still, guys!" Coach said. "I'm going to open my door and you do the same, Barney, but nobody move."

Very slowly he opened his door, and by inches he pulled himself out, then said, "Jake, slide out. Be careful now!"

Jake slid out to stand beside Coach, and then Coach said, "Take my hand, Barney."

I took his hand and held onto Joe with my other hand. Coach was pulling me out slowly, when suddenly there was a loud *crack!* The tree must have snapped, because the Bronco suddenly lurched away. All that saved Joe and me was Coach pulling us out with one hand!

"Dale! Boys!" Miss Jean screamed. She saw the Bronco plunge off the edge, and I don't think she could see us in the dark.

"It's all right, Jean!" Coach said at once. "We're all here."

We heard the crashing as the Bronco bounced off outcroppings of rocks and trees, and finally after a while it stopped.

"Thank God!" Miss Jean said as we made our way up to her. "You could have been killed!"

"We sure could, and it would have been my fault." Coach looked haggard and pale.

We stood there, and I could tell that he felt terrible. "Aw, Coach, you ought to practice what you preach."

"What?"

"You're always quoting that verse to me—the one that says: 'In everything give thanks.' " I grinned at him and said, "Well, put up or shut up!"

He stared at me and finally a little grin touched his lips. He sighed and shook his head saying, "You're going to be a handful to raise, Barney Buck!"

"But we are thankful," Miss Jean said. "It was a miracle that you didn't go over the edge!"

"That's right," Jake said. "But that's not the only thing you have to be thankful for."

All of us looked at him, and he grinned from ear to ear. "The next thing to be thankful for is that you don't have to spend your honeymoon on this lonesome old mountain all alone."

There was a moment's silence. Then Dale said, "Why, I don't think—"

"How are we going to get down from this roost?" Jake said, spreading his hands out. "There's no phone. We don't have a car. We can't walk down that road in the middle of the night, can we? And if it keeps snowing like this all night, it'll be a foot deep in the morning!"

"Nope, I guess we'll just have to have a *family* honeymoon, folks!"

Joe giggled and said, "I don't mind."

Then I glanced at Coach's face and I laughed too. "In *everything* give thanks, *Dad!*"

I guess when I called him *Dad* that sort of made a difference. I'd never done that before now, and it not only felt good to *me*, I saw that he liked it, too!

Would you believe all five of us got hysterical standing there in the snow, marooned in a cabin with no way down? It was the funniest thing any of us had ever seen.

Dad reached over and grabbed me and Jake, and then Joe and Mom pulled in close. We went around in that snow hollering and singing and scaring just about every possum in the country.

Finally, we all fell in the snow and had a snow fight. I got a mouth full of pine needles in the process, and we just made fools of ourselves.

Then when we were all out of breath, Dad stood up and said, "All right, wife, into the house."

Then he looked at Joe and Jake and me and said with a smile that lit up his whole face, "And I want every son of mine to stop this nonsense this minute. You hear me?"

I looked at Joe and Jake, and we all grinned and said, "Sure, Dad. Come on, Mom. Let's get in the house."

Five was the perfect number for a honeymoon, after all.

THIRTEEN
Sometimes
It Happens!

Maybe Jake and Joe and I thought five was
the right number for a honeymoon, but I
guess Coach and Miss Jean felt a little
different. Oh, they didn't *say* anything, but
when we heard an engine roaring up the road
about an hour after we lost the Bronco, they
both lit up like Christmas trees!

"Hey!" Coach yelled as he looked out the
window into the darkness. "That's a Cat
someone's driving up the road!"

We all piled out of the house just in time to
see a small Caterpillar tractor pull up. Even
before it stopped, Tippi jumped to the ground
and cried, "Happy honeymoon!"

"Tippi!" I said, "how in the world. . . !"

Her eyes were sparkling, and she looked
pretty caught in the beams of the headlights.
"It's my wedding present to you!" She smiled
at Coach and Miss Jean and added, "Since I

made such a mess out of the cake, I wanted to do something to make up for it." Then she grinned at me and added, ". . . Like getting these three out of your way so you can have a *real* honeymoon!"

"She thought it all up her ownself!"

We'd almost forgotten the driver of the Cat, but it was Tiny! He hopped down, his face nearly split in a grin. Looking down at Tippi, he said, "I told her you all wouldn't be able to get down with this snow, so she kept at me till I borrowed Mr. Simmons's tractor and here we are!"

Miss Jean ran over and hugged both of them, which was hard because Tiny was so big and Tippi was so little. "I think you're both wonderful!" she cried.

Coach got into the act, too. He grabbed all three of them and hollered, "Hooray for both of you kids!" Then he looked up with that twinkle in his eye that meant he was really happy and said, "Are you sure you're not angels in disguise?"

Jake was scowling. "Well, for crying out loud!" he said in disgust. "You'd think the three of us were communists or something! All this fuss over an ole honeymoon!" He kicked at the snow and stuck his hands in his pockets. "If you don't want us around for a couple of days, how you gonna put up with us for the rest of our lives?"

Right away Miss Jean's smile faded, and she went to Jake, put her arms around him, and said, "Oh, Jake, I didn't mean to sound like we didn't want you! I was just worried about being marooned up here!"

"Oh, don't pay any attention to him, Miss Jean," I said. "He's just too young to understand these things."

Jake stared at me like Geronimo in one of his bad moods. I usually watched out for him, but this time I went too far.

"He's just a kid, and you can't expect a kid to. . . . Hey! Watch out!"

Jake was about half my height, but built like a fire plug. He ran at me and hit me right in the belt buckle, and both of us went skittering across the snow and right over the edge where we'd lost the Bronco!

Jake was yelling and screaming in my ear and still trying to sock me. I was trying to grab a sapling to stop us from falling off the end of the world. I could hear everyone else calling frantically, but I got a mouthful of snow when I opened my mouth to holler back.

After a few flips and an encounter or two with some of the stone outcroppings that raked some of the skin off my hand, we finally hit a good-sized pin oak and stopped. Jake took the worst of it, catching it right in his stomach, and then I fell against him. He said, "Wuff!" and quit hollering.

"Barney! Jake! Are you all right?"

Almost by the time we got stopped, Coach came sliding down the bank and rammed right into my back, which took away my

170

breath. So with both Jake and me speechless, Coach did all the talking—which he would have done anyway!

He yanked me up with one hand and Jake with the other, then whispered fiercely, "You two clowns get back up that hill! And if I hear one word—just *one*—I'll begin your education on what a father's role is when two knotheads act like spoiled brats!"

"One word about what?" Jake asked meekly. He'd never seen Coach looking so stern, and I hadn't either.

"About anything unpleasant! You've already upset your mother, and I won't have it, you hear me?"

Well, it was funny. I mean, there we were hanging onto the side of a frozen cliff in the middle of the night. We'd just made perfect donkeys out of ourselves, and Coach was hopping mad at us. By rights we should have been feeling pretty miserable.

But I wasn't. A quick glance at Jake told me he wasn't either. He had a smile on his broad face. It was because Coach had said, "Your mother. . . ."

It was so good to hear that! I thought I'd gotten over not having a mother, but right then I knew that I really hadn't! I guess if you lose an arm, you get to where you don't notice it so much; but then there must be times when you realize that you're not the same as you used to be.

It was cold as anything out there on that

slope, but I suddenly felt very warm. "I'm sorry, Dad," I said. "Let's go up and I'll tell Mom how sorry I am."

Jake nodded and said quickly, "Yeah, I wouldn't want Mom to worry—not on her honeymoon, would I, Pop?"

"Don't call me *Pop!*" But even though his face was still a little stiff, as our new dad looked at us, I saw he wasn't missing what was happening. He gave us both a fast hug, and since he was the strongest man in town, he just about broke all my ribs, but I didn't care! "You two clowns are going to have to be educated!" he said, but then he smiled that good smile of his and added, "All right, up you go!"

When we got back up to the level ground, we were welcomed like explorers lost in the Arctic for a month! Mom kept trying to hug us both and saying motherly kinds of stuff, and Tiny insisted on shaking hands with us over and over. Since he had a grip like a Stilson wrench, I lost all feeling in my right hand for an hour! Joe was jumping up and down and hollering like crazy, and Tippi grabbed me in a bear hug and whispered, "Oh, Barney, I was so afraid you'd be hurt!"

To tell the truth, that made me feel pretty important. I was beginning to wish I *had* broken something!

Finally Dad said, "Well, let's go inside."

"Inside!" Tippi said in surprise. "We didn't

come up here to add two *more* to your honeymoon."

"But you can't do anything tonight!" Mom said.

"Sure we can," Tiny grinned. "We can load up and leave you and the mister to your honeymooning."

Mom got a little pink and looked at Dad helplessly.

"All five of you can't ride that thing down the mountain," Dad said.

"Shore we can, Mister Littlejohn," Tiny said with a grin. "May have to sit on laps or something. . . ."

"Hey, I have an idea!" Joe slapped his leg and shouted, "We can pull the Bronco up with the Cat!"

I caught on right away and said, "That's it! There's a big winch and a long cable on the back. All we have to do is hook onto the Bronco and Tiny can pull it up!"

"In the dark?" Tippi asked, looking down the slope.

"You know, it might work," Dad said slowly. "We'd have to get a wrecker anyway, and that Cat has more power. I'll take the hook down and when I get it attached, you take it up real slow, Tiny."

"I'll go with you, Dad," I said quickly. Tiny backed the Cat up to the side of the bluff and dad took the cable with the hook and we started slowly down the cliff.

"Be careful, Dale!" Mom called as we made our way down.

"And you, too, Barney!" Tippi added.

Actually, it wasn't too bad. The Bronco hadn't gone as far as we'd thought, and by chance it was upright with the front pointed right up the mountain.

"Looks like it didn't even roll over," Dad said with relief. He got the hook attached and got inside behind the wheel. Then he said, "You'd better not get in, Barney."

"Aw, Dad, let me come!" I begged. "I want to be with you."

He hesitated, then grinned. "Well, I guess it'll be all right."

I hopped in and he added, "Don't think you're going to be able to manipulate me all the time!"

"I know, Dad, but this is special."

Dad nodded. "It sure is, son." Then he stuck his head out the window and yelled, "All right. Take it slow, Tiny!"

The Bronco gave a lurch, then slowly started up the slope. Dad and I were both a little tense, but it went fine! We crested the rise and got out and there was another welcome for us, wouldn't you know?

"Now you all can come down soon as the snow melts," Tiny said, nodding his head. "Maybe a week or two, but I guess since you're on your honeymoon, it don't make no nevermind, does it, Mister Littlejohn?"

"Why, I don't think. . . !" Dad was about as

pink as Mom by that time, so I took pity on them.

"Let's get going, you guys. Mom, we'll see you and Dad when you come down." I gave her a hug and a kiss, and Jake and Joe crowded around for the same. Then I got us all packed on the seat of the Cat. Tiny was driving, and somehow Joe wound up sitting in the little space behind the seat. Jake was wedged in between Tiny and me, and Tippi was sitting on my lap.

We waved good-bye, and Tiny headed down the steep road. It was really fun, not dangerous at all with the Caterpillar. One of those things would climb up a telephone pole if it could get a hold, and there's no way you can turn one over.

It even had a radio; so Jake insisted on listening to one of his idiot rock groups on FM 100. I usually argued with him, but with Tippi sitting on my lap I couldn't say too much.

She was trying to tell me something, but the music was so loud that she had to put her lips close to my ear. She was saying something about her father, but to tell the truth I was so nervous with her on my lap that I couldn't understand what it was.

Finally we got down off the mountain, and there was my pickup. "I didn't think you'd want to ride all the way home on the tractor," Tippi said, "so I had your truck brought here."

"Gee, that's swell, Tippi," I said as we got out. My legs were so numb I nearly fell down. "Come on, you guys. Let's get moving."

Jake and Joe both wanted to ride the Cat back to the house with Tiny, so I said, "Well, you come right on. Tiny, thanks a million!"

Tiny beamed and took off fast on the level ground—fast for a Caterpillar, that is.

Tippi and I got in the truck, and we passed them with a wave. "Tiny is sure a nice fellow," I said.

Tippi was quiet for a time. Then she said, "Yes. You taught me about how to like people, Barney."

"Well, anyway, what were you saying about your dad, Tippi?"

She moved over to sit closer to me—or maybe just to get closer to the old heater in the floor. "Barney, I've been so jealous of you!"

"Jealous?"

"Yes, of the family you're going to have."

"But Tippi, you've got your father, and he's a fine man."

"I know. Dad's sweet, but he's—well, he's so busy with his work I never see him much."

"Well, he *is* a little that way," I admitted.

"Yes, and I was so jealous of what you and Jake and Joe were going to have with neat parents like Dale Littlejohn and Jean Fletcher. But it's all right now, Barney."

"It is?"

"Oh, yes, and I'm so happy!"

She reached over and took my arm and held it, and I asked, "What's happened, Tippi?"

"I'm not going to tell you, Barney," she said with a smile, "but I'll *show* you!"

"You will?"

"Yes, as soon as we get to your house."

I tried to find out more, but she just sat there and smiled and only kept saying, "You'll see."

We got to our house, and all the lights were on in every room.

"What in the world is going on?" I asked as we stopped and got out of the truck.

"It's a party!" Tippi pulled me toward the door and added, "Your mom wanted her sister to stay here until the honeymoon was over, and Ellen asked a few people over."

"A *few* people!" I exclaimed. "Looks like she invited half of Clark County!"

We went in and the living room was *packed!* I knew lots of the people, but there were some that I'd never seen. "They're Ellen's friends from the city," Tippi whispered.

I glanced around, wondering where old Mrs. Taylor was. No way could she be sleeping through this noise. "Where's Mrs. Taylor?" I asked.

"Oh, she's gone to live with the sheriff and his wife," Tippi explained.

That was good news for Mrs. Taylor, who'd been having a hard time managing us boys.

And it was great news for us, because now we had a real mom and dad and wouldn't need her help anymore!

"Why, Barney, you're back!" Miss Ellen came up and gave me a hug, which surprised me, and then she gave Tippi one, too. "Where are your brothers?" she asked.

"They're coming back with Tiny on the Cat," Tippi said. She looked around and said, "What a nice party!"

A man in grey trousers and a Scottish plaid jacket came over and said, "Glad to see you made it safely, Barney. I was worried."

For a second I wondered why he would be worried when I didn't even know him. Then I turned to face him and took a closer look.

"Professor Vandiver!" I stared at him, and I guess my jaw must have dropped a foot. "Why, I didn't recognize you!"

Tippi gave me a little pinch on the arm that hurt and said quickly, "Oh, Barney, don't be silly!"

She pulled me away, but not before I saw Ellen glide over to the professor and give him a smooth smile. She took his arm and led him over to a couple of her friends, and I heard her say, "Jon and Frances, this is Professor Vandiver you've been wanting to meet. . . ."

"What's going on?" I demanded as soon as Tippi and I got away to stand by the refreshment table. "What's happened to your dad?"

Tippi asked with a sort of twinkle in her eye, "Don't you see?"

"Well, I see he's got on clothes that fit and his hair is cut."

She shook her head and made a face, "Men are blind!"

That got to me a little and I said, "Well, what is it then? What's the big secret?"

She came up close and said, "Lean down so I can whisper." When I did she whispered, "They're going to get married!"

"What!" I almost shouted. Then when she shushed me, I said, "Are you serious? When did he ask her to marry him? I mean, they've only known each other a few days!"

"Oh, he hasn't *asked* her yet, of course. But it's all settled."

I stared at her. "You're rowing with one oar, Tippi! Why, people don't get married like that!"

She gave me a funny, secret smile and pulled me over to sit beside her in a corner of the room.

"Let me explain it to you, Barney," she said. "Daddy isn't a ladies' man. Mother told me she had to practically hand him a list of things a man must do to get a wife. But she loved him and he really loved her. She just had to help him with the things that go into a courtship."

I stared across the room at the professor. He looked terrific and there was an air about him I'd never seen. "He looks different."

"He *is* different, Barney," Tippi said. "Daddy needs a wife, and Ellen needs a husband. She's a little snooty, but she'll be different now. I had a long talk with her yesterday, and we understand each other, I think." She turned her face to watch her father and Ellen, then said, "I think six months would be long enough, don't you, Barney?"

I stared at her. "You told me once you could manipulate people, Tippi. Is this a sample?"

Then all of a sudden Tippi's eyes filled up with tears, and she gave a sob. "I'm going to cry. Get me out of here, Barney!"

We got up, and I led her out the side door onto the screened-in porch. It was cold, but private.

She turned to me and said with a break in her voice, "I've been so lonesome, Barney. Daddy has his work, but I–I *need* more than that."

"But. . . !"

"I know what you're thinking, but you don't know Daddy," she said. "He's been perfectly *miserable* since Mother died. Some awful women almost trapped him, but I saw through them. Daddy's a famous man and has a little money, and that's all they wanted."

"But you don't know anything about Ellen!"

"Yes, I do!" She took my arm and said fiercely, "She's almost thirty years old and is frightened that she'll never find a husband, that no man wants her. And she's really sweet, Barney, like Jean."

I thought about that. "I noticed that, Tippi. But do you really think they'll fall in love?"

"I'm *praying* they will," she whispered. Then she looked up at me, tears running down her face. "Didn't you say God will answer our prayers, Barney?"

Well, she had me there!

"Sure, but. . . ."

She gave kind of a shudder and then really began to cry. She leaned against me, and her face was muffled against my chest as she said, "We all need each other so much!"

I never knew what to do with a crying girl on my hands. So I patted her shoulder and was just about to say something, when a voice said, "Well, *excuse* me!"

I glanced up and there was Debra, looking mad enough to bite a nail in two!

She did an about-face and started off, but I grabbed her and dragged her out to the porch.

"Now, just a minute, Debra. This isn't what it looks like!" I argued.

"No? What is it actually?"

Debra's voice was about twenty degrees colder than the snow on the ground.

"Barney, go away. I want to talk to Debra," Tippi said, coming behind us.

I was glad enough to let her do the explaining and made my getaway into the house. Professor Vandiver saw me and came over with Ellen beside him. He had a smile on his face, and I was amazed at what a nice-looking man he was all cleaned up.

"I have some good news for you, Barney," he said.

"Good news?"

"The relics from the digging, you remember?"

"Oh, yes." They seemed like ancient history. "What about them, Professor?"

"Your share of the proceeds will come to a little over two thousand dollars."

I stared at him, wondering if I'd heard him right. "Two thousand dollars!"

Miss Ellen touched his arm, and said, "Socrates has been so anxious to see you boys make some money, Barney! Jean told me you have a college fund, and this should help."

"And I'm hoping that we'll be able to help you get into a good school, Barney, when that time comes." He took Ellen's hand and smiled at her. "Ellen and I have been making some plans about that, haven't we?"

"Indeed we have."

She gave him a smile that would have melted the paint off a radio tower and led him away.

He's a gone coon! I said to myself. But I saw it would be a great thing if it worked out.

"Barney."

I turned around and there was Debra. Tippi was making her way across the room to her father and Ellen, and she gave me a high sign and a wink as she caught my eye.

"I've decided to forgive you," Debra said.

"Forgive me!" I yelped. "Forgive me for *what?*"

Debra Simmons was growing up to be a woman, no doubt about that! She stood there giving me one of her heavy-lidded looks, tapping her chin with one finger, and making me feel guilty as sin . . . and I hadn't even done anything!

She took me by the arm and said, "You can take me for refreshments, Barnabas. After that we'll go have a nice little talk about how you mustn't let yourself go onto screened-in porches with any girls except me."

Well, what was I going to do?

"Debra, I am innocent!" I pleaded.

She laughed and said, "I know it, and I intend to keep you that way!"

As we ate our cake, I said, "It's funny how everything turned out swell, isn't it, Debra? I mean, we got the money from the dig, we had a great wedding, and Tippi and her dad and Miss Ellen are probably gonna be fine. Why, it's like the stories that end up saying, '. . . And they lived happily ever after!' "

Debra gave me a pretty smile and said, "Well, Barney, sometimes it happens that way!"

And so it does!